TO BE FREE!

TO BE FREE!

A Novel By

RON MARTIN

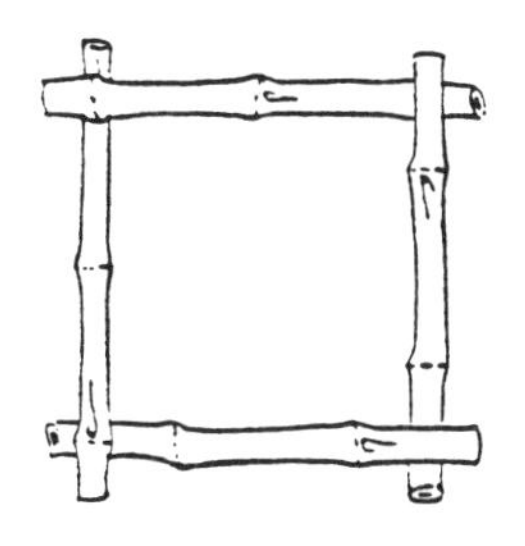

THE VANGUARD PRESS

NEW YORK

Published by Vanguard Press, Inc.,
424 Madison Avenue, New York, N.Y. 10017.
Published simultaneously in Canada by Book Center, Inc.,
Montreal, Quebec.

Library of Congress Cataloging-in-Publication Data

Martin, Ron, 1941–
To be free!

1. Vietnamese Conflict, 1961–1975—Fiction. I. Title.
PS3563.A7282T6 1986 813′.54 86-9052
ISBN 0-8149-0925-6

Designer: Tom Bevans
Manufactured in the United States of America.

To those
who did not return.
To those who did return,
wounded in body
and in spirit.

PROLOGUE

ANY MAN could be broken. Ramsey knew that. It just took time to find the hidden fears. They had the time and he had the fears, secreted deep in the fragile corners of his mind. He had already given more than was required. Admittedly, the information was false, but the memory brought a vile taste of shame and despondency.

The wall he had built to fortify himself was crumbling. They were getting close. He had to get out. The rains were coming any day now; that would be the best time. Things went slack; they let their guard down in the monotony of the monsoon.

This was his last chance. His physical condition had deteriorated to the point that made his survival on an arduous escape attempt questionable. The once heavily muscled frame had shed some thirty pounds during his period of captivity. Pale blue eyes stared from deep within their sockets. The ragged, dirty blond hair, held in place by a sweat-stained bandana, was becoming sparse and thin. His body was covered with oozing sores from which his strength seemed to drain day by day.

He sat in the corner of the bamboo cage. From his vantage point he could visualize the journey beginning. Down the grassy slope into the jungle. The descent, hidden by the thick canopy, to the valley floor and the river. His eyes traced the course of the river, drawn to the faint gleam of the sea in the distance.

As far back as he could remember, the sea had represented freedom. He supposed most men held that romantic notion. Only those men who worked the sea knew differently. Now, more than ever, he had to reach the sea. Even if he died there, at least he would, in some measure, be free.

The glimmer was gone, the features of the valley and river becoming indistinct as daylight faded. Another day filled with pain, hunger, and now isolation. How many days had there been, he wondered?

In the beginning he had struggled to record the

passage of days, weeks, and months. Sometime after the sixth month he stopped. It didn't seem important anymore. The goal was to get through each day, not remember its name or number.

In the bush, calendars were kept with fanatical accuracy. Each day eliminated with ceremonial flourish. One day less, one day closer to that Silverbird for the Real World.

The first crack had appeared in his wall with the neglect of time. When he had allowed the days to pass, blending together, something was lost. He wasn't quite sure what it was, but a hollow sense of resignation enveloped him like a fog sifting over the landscape.

Night settled around him, the sounds of darkness went unheard. He labored, trying to turn his eyes inward, seeking visual images of the beginning....

1
THE MISSION

THREE MEN dressed in tiger-stripe fatigues slid quietly through the dense foliage. They moved cautiously, yards apart, Ramsey at the point. The air was heavy, filled with moisture. They had traveled south all day, coming out of the hills.

It had been painfully slow going. Ramsey had studiously avoided any path or track, keeping them concealed in the heavy vegetation. The ambushes they had set up achieved nothing except the squandering of precious time.

But they were back there, stalking them, dogging

their trail. The little men in black pajamas were endlessly patient. They would wait until the advantage was all theirs, at the moment you were sure you had it made. Then they would strike.

Ramsey knew when it would be. He had almost become like the enemy, anticipating, crawling inside their minds. If it had been otherwise, the team would not have survived. Twenty-seven days in their country, moving every forty-eight hours.

The mission was simple. After insertion, proceed to the vicinity of the lower reaches of the Ho Chi Minh Trail. Report all movements and call in fire missions to the appropriate units. All the firepower in the world at their disposal and still the enemy kept coming. B-52s, 16-inch guns from naval gunfire, 105 mm and 155 mm howitzers, and still they came.

The enemy had known from the start the team was there. Only Ramsey's constant movement confused the North Vietnamese. Near the end the mission had been amended. They were ordered to retreat south toward Hill 881 North, searching for evidence of enemy buildup against the combat base at Khe Sanh.

Now, as they approached the landing zone for extraction, Ramsey sensed the pursuers closing the gap. He halted, frozen in midstride, then slowly folded himself into the ground. Martinez crouched, facing left. Harlow dropped, turning right into ambush position.

The landing zone was a half mile ahead, a clearing no more than a hundred yards square. Viewed from above, a postage-stamp island blasted out of the green landscape. The chopper was scheduled for 1730 hours. If Ramsey signaled a hot landing zone, they would have to walk out—another three days at least.

He lay listening, watching the valley below. Sweat squeezed from every pore of his body. He wearily lowered his head onto folded arms. It's too much, he thought. Twenty-seven days and nights in the boonies, living on meager rations and whatever they could scrounge from the land.

Now I know they're waiting. As soon as the chopper makes touchdown, they'll be there. Out of the bush, AK-47s blasting the crap out of us. Still, like a hero of some ancient tragedy, Ramsey knew he had to try. They moved off slowly down the slope.

Pham waited until the jungle absorbed Harlow's retreating figure. He rose and signaled the squad to follow. Pham was exhilarated. They must be close to the landing zone. Not only the team, but a helicopter would be his, a reward for the lengthy chase.

Fifty yards from the clearing, Ramsey halted. He indicated that Harlow and Martinez should proceed to the edge of the landing zone. As Harlow passed, Ramsey mimicked a radio transmission. Harlow nodded. Ramsey settled into a small depression on the left of the trail. From his position in the elephant grass he could observe most of the slope dropping to the valley floor.

They would be almost on top of him before he fired. Coming down out of the jungle onto the plain, they would be confused. They would not be able to tell how many gunners were concealed by the tall grass. It might provide enough time for the bird to get in and out.

Pham moved his men into a horseshoe-shaped formation. They advanced slowly, slipping through the rain forest. Pham tried to visualize the coming firefight. The Marines would try to secure the landing zone, leaving behind an ambush. The two sides of the horseshoe would bypass the ambush. If they drew fire, the gunner would be located for the closed end of the formation. While they engaged, the rest of the squad would move forward, closer to the clearing, and prepare to destroy the helicopter.

Ramsey appeared to be asleep. He was not. Intent, listening, he watched a red ant carry a sliver of bamboo across his field of fire. Only his eyes moved, sweeping from side to side. His body tensed. He picked up the distant sound of rotor blades. It was the sound of Vietnam. Forever after, the distinctive sound would make his eyelids sweat and tighten his thighs, ready for movement.

Pham listened also. They had reached the edge of the grass bordering the valley floor. A small trail, perhaps a yard wide, snaked through the high grass toward the clearing. He had to be careful now. He could lose it all. Where was the ambush? He could wait until the chopper was down and then move quickly through the grass. Perhaps move now, surround the clearing. Maybe there was no ambush. It was possible the Marines didn't know the squad was so close. The team would be vulnerable. This close to a firefight, actions became hasty and rapid. Pham decided to move.

The chopper was getting close. It would come in fast, not even touch down. They would throw themselves into the ship under covering fire from the door gunner.

Two or three minutes and we're on our way, thought Ramsey. Then he spotted them, off to his right, maybe thirty yards, an almost imperceptible swaying of the grass. He swung his eyes left, searching. There it was again, about the same distance. He slid his hand down to the small satchel of grenades.

The launcher lay in front of him and, by his right side, an M-16. The faint pop of Harlow's green smoke grenade was Ramsey's signal. He quickly loaded, pointed to his left, and fired. The muffled cough of the grenade launcher had barely faded before he fired again, this time to the right. The first round impacted. Ramsey fired again, straight to his front. He rolled to his left, rose and ran, changing direction every three steps, deeper into the grass.

As the chopper came in, the door gunner opened up, ranging in on the exploding grenades. Ramsey kept firing, pumping grenades out in all directions. Moving, always moving, he dropped the launcher and burned off a magazine from the M-16 through the grass. He retreated toward the clearing.

Pham was disoriented. Fire was coming from everywhere—the helicopter, the grass. He screamed orders moving his men toward the landing zone. Three were hit and down; others lay in the grass, frozen in place by the incoming rounds. He ran frantically, kicking and cursing, urging his men to concentrate fire on the helicopter.

They were peasants, not hard-core, Pham thought, smashing his rifle butt into the side of a cowering youngster. Ramsey's last grenade had shredded the legs and stomach of Duc. A random shot, lucky. Now he sat staring, incredulous at the blue-red ooze seeping through fingers clasped over his midsection.

Every nerve in Ramsey's body jumped and exploded like an electrical short circuit. They had located his position. Rounds were whipping through the grass, whispering death. Back he went, waiting until the last possible moment to make his run.

Martinez and Harlow threw themselves aboard, splattered by hot shell casings from the M-60 the door gunner traversed back and forth. They turned to see Ramsey finally on the trail, sprint for the clearing. Rounds like a riveter's gun hammered along the side of the chopper. The door gunner catapulted back, a face transformed to blood and bone. The bird started to lift.

Ramsey was twenty yards away. Then, like a half-moon, he bowed, arms outstretched, and collapsed. The pilot took the chopper into a hard right, climbing turn. Harlow would forever hold the frame of Ramsey's upturned face, mouth open, teeth bared, fists clenched in helpless rage....

2
SWANSON

THE IMAGE of the helicopter faded into an impassively dying sun. Ramsey stood, grasping the bars of his cage. Insects swarmed around the bowed head. He could not stand erect. They wouldn't even give him that much. The cage was five feet high, too short by one foot for his height.

He recalled a movie showing survivors of the concentration camps of World War II. The emaciation of his body reminded him of their appearance. He slyly patted scraps of vegetables secreted at his waistband.

When it was fully dark, he would bury them with the other supplies, ready for the journey.

There was one other cage on the slope down from the main camp. It was currently occupied by Swanson, an Army Ranger captured near Hang Vei. He, like Ramsey, was a troublemaker. They had formed a common code of resistance. Of the eight men at the camp, these two had more cage time than all the others put together.

Swanson was black. They had tried to use this, but Swanson wouldn't listen. He was a tremendously proud man. The resistance was for himself, not for God or country, but purely because he believed in Swanson.

Tran, the interrogator, had tried to pit Ramsey and Swanson against each other. The winner had been promised extra rations and slack time. They had both stood, smiling at each other. Tran danced around them, goading, prodding, and finally beating them with a long bamboo stick.

Later, in their isolation, twenty-five yards apart, they laughed and gestured obscenely to each other between the bars of the cages. They barely knew each other. Communication was limited to furtive whispering, in the field cutting brush, during propaganda meetings, tapping on cell walls. They recognized in each other a strength, a need to survive, a vow not to get fucked over, to get out alive.

Ramsey wished he could let Swanson in on his

plan. It would be impossible. The only lengthy communication was by wall-tapping. The others would learn of his plan. One of the weak sisters might trade the information. The guards beat any violator of the silence rule. Psychologically, it was effective strategy.

That's how it had been in boot camp. You're alone and you think no one is suffering as much or so alone. As a group you could resist collectively, but alone what can you achieve? Then, if you screw up, the group suffers and turns on you like parasites, encouraged by drill instructors or the enemy.

In his time at the camp, Ramsey had learned to endure the animosity directed toward him by some of his fellow prisoners. His defiance had caused smaller rations, longer work days, and occasional vicious beatings for the group.

Now he was not sure if he had the strength to make the attempt. With Swanson there would be a much better chance. His leg ached from the round he had taken back at the clearing so long ago....

3

PHAM

He had been so close. The open hatch, Harlow and Martinez screaming and firing. Suddenly he was kicked from behind, thrown forward face down in the grass. A fireball shot through the back of his thigh, groin, and belly. Dust and sweat clogged his mouth. He tried to rise. The leg refused to support his weight. Ramsey strained, straightened arms lifting his torso from the ground.

The dust and debris whipped by spinning rotors stung his face. His two companions were framed in the rectangular door opening. Martinez was firing, Harlow screaming at the helmeted head of the pilot. The pitch of the rotors rose. Skids lifted, the nose dipped, and the ship swung away, severing Ramsey's thin filament of hope.

"No! You can't leave me! Come back, you bastards, come back!" he screamed, filled with rage and despair. The screams became sobs. Ramsey crumpled and lay still.

They came slowly, gathering around the fallen man. Pham went berserk. He leaped forward, kicking and gouging at every portion of Ramsey's body. Ramsey covered his head. Boots and rifle butts sought to pulverize him into the ground.

His clasped fingers behind his head were smashed. Feet now concentrated on the uncovered area. Grasping hands wrenched him over onto his back. The blows were now aimed at his stomach, face, and groin. Flashes of iridescence exploded in his brain. A boot stomped down on his testicles. Teeth and lips splintered and split, a rifle barrel was thrust into his mouth. Blood and vomit spewed from the shattered cavity.

He drifted in and out on waves of nausea. What a shitty way to go, he thought. Finally, mercifully, he was gone, entering some neutral state where the pain was dull, subdued.

His eyes came unglued slowly, blinking like some animal after long hibernation. Pain was everywhere. He forced his eyes to focus on the surroundings. They sat squatting, fingers scooping rice from makeshift containers. He was ignored, a distasteful remnant of some forgotten engagement.

Pham saw Ramsey was awake. Slowly, deliberately, he stood, unscrewing the top of his canteen. The Asian face was fragmented. Contempt was there, but also a tinge of respect. He poured the contents over the battered visage. Ramsey's mouth worked frantically, licking and sucking the liquid into his parched body.

Pham turned and issued a series of commands. Two squad members roughly tied Ramsey's feet and wrists with thin strips of cloth. A long bamboo pole was thrust between his wrists and ankles. Like some victim of the hunt, he was hoisted, hanging upside down, by two of the soldiers.

If he were asked to recall the next few hours or even days, Ramsey would be at a loss. He remained conscious for short periods, fueled by rage and jolted by the agony spreading throughout his body. When the pain became no longer bearable, he screamed and cursed obscenely at his captors. Finally gagged, he lapsed into blackness.

The round had passed through the back of his thigh and exited cleanly. No major artery had been hit, but the wound constantly oozed dark red blood.

The squad left the valley floor and climbed north through the rain forest. They halted sometime during the night. Ramsey could not be sure how long, or how far, they had traveled. He lost all sense of time and merely strove to endure.

At the halt they dropped him roughly to the ground and untied his wrists. One of them gave him cold tea and a rice ball. They sat watching without expression. His numb fingers tried to bring the tea to his mouth. The precious liquid slopped down his chin and chest. The first mouthful he used to rinse, spitting bits of skin and teeth. He greedily sucked the remaining fluid into his dehydrated body.

The rice he couldn't eat. The nausea and turmoil of his stomach could not accept anything solid. He knew the food was necessary, but his eyes closed, shutting out the nightmare. Dimly he was aware of the wrist bindings being replaced.

As his mind shut down, a brief smile slid across the tortured face. "Sleep that knits up the ravell'd sleave of care." The quote flickered across his mind and vanished. Not this time, mother, he thought, you're in deep, deep shit. Another halt, then on the move again, before dawn. Ramsey dozed fitfully. Now, once more, they strung him on the pole.

His limbs ached and throbbed. The wound tore open. He began to build his resolve. Somewhere deep in his gut a voice began chanting, "Fuck 'em, fuck 'em all. I will survive. I will survive."

With insane relish he ground broken teeth together as they swung through the pale light filtering down from the canopy of green. They crossed a sluggish, muddy river. Ramsey was plunged under the turbid water. An intense, gripping claustrophobia enveloped his being. He arched his body, seeking light and air. All he could think of was the dirty, stinking water flowing around his wound. Gangrene, gangrene, the terrible word reverberated through his brain.

At last he surfaced, taking great, harsh gasps of air. The soldiers laughed at his feeble struggles. A leech had fixed itself on his lower back. Ramsey could feel its relentless squirming as it dug into his skin. Its black, gross body would glut with his blood.

On they went, ever north, through the steaming rain forest. At times Ramsey was vaguely aware of his surroundings. The swinging of the dark green covering, pierced by shafts of light, had a hypnotic effect. The torment of his anguished muscles was temporarily subdued. He could sense the rise and fall of the terrain from the angle of his body.

The squad moved on in silence. Soldiers assigned to carry the prisoner switched often, without halting progress. Late in the day a light observer aircraft approached their route of march. Ramsey was thrown off the trail into the brush. His captors scattered. There was little chance of being spotted.

They remained concealed until the engine noise had faded into the twilight. Pham called a halt. Once his wrists were free and fingers able to function, Ramsey sought the leech imbedded in his flesh. A malicious grin creased the face of a soldier. He withdrew a long jungle knife and with the flat of the blade smashed the leech against Ramsey's back. Ramsey doubled over, head between knees. His empty stomach heaved and convulsed.

Later he forced down some tea and a handful of sticky rice. Once again the enemy squatted around, watching, observing his reaction to the humiliation. He smiled and began to speak: "Well, what do you think, you little fuckers? At least I got four of you, Charlie. How does that grab you, you dog turds?"

They grinned at one another, all except Pham. He sensed the derision in Ramsey's voice. A foot caught Ramsey in the throat. He collapsed backward, struggling frantically for air. Stifling a sob, he sucked oxygen through his nose.

They resumed the march. Toward midnight they moved into a hamlet. There was no indication that the villagers were awake or noticed their arrival. The ten or so crude hooches scattered around the clearing remained darkened.

Ramsey's porters entered a hut and dropped him unceremoniously on the earthen floor. One of the soldiers remained, presumably to act as a guard. He sat in the open doorway, facing into the hut.

Ramsey raised his bound wrists toward the guard, nodding his head up and down. The man ignored him, gazing at some distant point on the far wall. Ramsey used his feet and elbows to arrange an acceptable position for his tortured body. He lay on his side, knees drawn up, arms folded under his head. The guard sat with his back against the door frame.

Soft light illuminated the village. Directly across from the hut the placid surface of a rice paddy shimmered, reflecting between the huts. The tranquil scene filled Ramsey with a deep melancholy longing. Tears rolled over his battered face.

He slept fitfully, dreaming of Cathy. Then there were dark swamps, filled with tracer fire. An old woman swam into his vision, her walnut face punctuated by vacant brown eyes and toothless mouth. She offered a bowl, a thin watery substance with floating bits of green.

The bowl touched his numbed fingers, she looked into his eyes. She lowered her head and dribbled a mouthful of spit into his meal. The skin around her eyes cracked like a dry river bed. She smiled innocently into his eyes.

Ramsey took the proffered bowl and, returning her gaze, emptied it greedily. He tossed the bowl into her lap. "Thanks, you old fart." He smiled and inclined his head graciously. She rose, shaking her head, and retreated into the gray dawn.

They came, untied his feet, and pushed him from the hut. The people of the village gathered, fixing the foreigner with hostile stares. They were either old or very young. They stood in the dusty trail bisecting the hamlet.

The children moved closer, encouraged by the soldiers and adults. Finally the boldest leaped forward and slapped at him with a long stick. Those who had hung back now joined the game with relish.

Ramsey staggered, trying to retain his balance. The blows sought to cut him down. He covered his head and rushed forward but was immediately beaten from behind. He turned, but they closed in again from all sides.

Suddenly they retreated, brushed aside by Pham. He grabbed the staggering Ramsey and led him to a small cart hitched behind a water buffalo. His feet were bound and he was pushed to the floor. The cart began moving slowly, rolling from side to side, matching the gait of the water buffalo.

Ramsey lay back in the grass covering the floor, thankful he did not have to face the horrible strain of being carried on the pole. Automatically, as he had done many times on various clandestine missions, he reviewed his situation.

They had obviously crossed the border into the North. The villagers had been openly hostile. They were using the cart, moving on an easily observable trail. The squad was strung out behind the cart, talking back and forth, relaxing and laughing. The column took on an almost holiday atmosphere.

The sun rose higher. Dust swirled in the cool air not yet heated by the ferocious sun. Birds and insects swooped around as they ambled along, keeping pace with the plodding buffalo. The trail passed through low foothills, twisting, turning, and rising with each passing hour.

Ramsey felt it was vitally important that he keep track of distance. It was essential to know where he was in relation to friendly territory. He guessed they were moving at no more than two or three miles an hour. There was no way he was going to Hanoi with this crew. They must be headed for some holding camp. Then, if he was good propaganda material, he would be shipped farther north.

His biggest worry was his body. If it began to break down, he was sure mental deterioration must follow. The leg was his greatest concern. Fingers of pain reached upward to his groin and farther down to the knee. The material of his fatigues was coagulated with blood and stuck to the wound. If he could remain immobile, the holes would close. But what kinds of crap would be inside?

When the sun was high, the column swung off the trail. Ramsey was reminded of a turnoff somewhere on Route 1, between San Francisco and Carmel. Behind, the jungle foliage sought to eclipse the small half-moon of sand. Beyond, across the trail, a long valley extended, shrouded in mist. At intervals the cover was punctured by small islands, the summits of green hills.

For the first time cooking fires were lit. He pushed himself up, watching the others eat. Pham pushed a bowl of hot liquid into his hands. Rice and vegetables floated on the surface. His shrunken stomach gratefully received the soup.

When he had finished, Pham motioned for him to lie back down. He began to cut through the leg of

Ramsey's fatigues. The cloth ripped quickly away from the wound. Ramsey closed his eyes, jaws clenched, sweat pouring from his body. Pham probed the edges of each hole, removing lumps of dried blood and fragments of shredded skin.

Pham rattled an order to the troops gathered around the cooking fires. One of the men rose, carrying a large can of steaming water from the fire. Ramsey's eyes grew wild with apprehension. Pham grasped the can by its wire handle, tipping the scalding water over both the entrance and exit wounds.

Ramsey screamed, fire shooting through his body. He hovered on the edge of red blackness, leg and belly burning. He was dimly aware of Pham binding his leg tightly with strips of cloth.

They moved out on the trail, swaying, rocking, gaining altitude with every hour. His leg dull and throbbing, Ramsey pondered the fact of Pham's crude medical assistance. He decided, not without some measure of hope, that he was a valuable prisoner. The enemy would dearly love information on the numerous long-range reconnaissance teams operating in the North.

The heat was now oppressive, all mist burned off from the valley below. The air was thinner as they climbed higher into the hills. To combat pain and fatigue, Ramsey pushed his mind somewhere beyond the physical realms of the body.

Now, the sun rising higher, he was on a long sandy

beach curving gracefully toward the hook of the Cape. Cathy lay beside him, hair the color of winter sun, splayed out behind her head. He was kissing the long slim neck and little hollows created by her collarbones.

The salty taste of her, the smell of baby oil, shut down the messages of pain radiating toward his brain. His fingers traced small circles from the inside of her knee upward to the smooth inside of her thigh. She murmured soft, low sounds, returning his kisses. Her arms came over his neck and shoulders, pulling him fully over her body.

He was jolted awake, muddy water swirled around the floor of the cart. They were in the middle of a river some thirty yards wide. The buffalo, water up to its chest, was bellowing, driven forward by a soldier wielding a long supple stick. On the far bank, Ramsey could see the beginnings of a small trail that snaked farther up into the mountain ridges.

The column emerged from the river. They moved on, the soldiers laughing and joking. From their manner Ramsey supposed the journey was almost over. He was right. A mile or so up the trail they came upon the camp....

4

THE DREAM

NIGHT HAD fully covered his cage. He could barely distinguish the low camp buildings. He willed sleep to come, his mind restless, filled with thoughts of the capture and the dream of escape. He reviewed the plan again.

It was basically simple. Everything depended on the rains. That, and his confinement during the beginnings of the monsoon. The upright supports of the cage were anchored, driven into the slope of the hill. The run-off at the height of a downpour loosened the earth around each vertical bamboo pole.

During one of his numerous sentences he had observed the rainwater swirling past, scooping out soil. He had aided the process, frantically digging around the base of a pole with his fingers.

Adrenalin pumping, an animal without reason, he tore at the earth—a demented soul, burrowing in the soil seeking a fragment of life. The aching fingers passed beneath the bamboo upright. He fell back exhausted. The plan was born.

Later, when the rains had gone and sanity returned, he filled the hole. Elated, he cultivated the growing embryo of the escape. He would need more than fingers. A trench, deep enough to allow his body passage under the vertical poles, would require time. He would have only a few hours. Once out, he must put distance between himself and the camp. Ramsey sat, nourishing the thought. It can be done! It can be done!

On his next punishment for a stubborn disobedience, he had smuggled in a digging stick. A brush-cutting detail gave him the opportunity. He chose a short, thick section of bamboo and concealed the tool along his forearm. The search by the guards at the conclusion of each day typically ignored the lower arms. They concentrated on armpits, groin, and legs.

Ramsey had stood, arms raised, breath held, as the guard concluded his cursory explorations.

The stick was buried, secreted in a corner of the cage. In another corner he had a cache of rice wrapped in cloth. He knew, logically, that the food would rot. But emotionally he chose to believe it would sustain his journey. At times of totally lucid thought, he considered himself insane.

Here he was, somewhere deep in the North. How could he possibly escape in his weakened state? What would he do when he reached the sea, swim home? Where there was the sea, there were fishermen. He would steal a boat and head south.

The dream had to be kept alive, a pinpoint of light in a dark world of pain and degradation. Ramsey now knew it was close, the beginning of the end. He could not foresee the ending, but he had to begin the resurrection of himself as a human being.

Many times he had thought of giving up, of giving them what they wanted. It would be so easy. A signed statement admitting to his war crimes. A brief televised appearance, denouncing the war as a capitalistic trap designed to enslave the worker.

He had heard the words so often from the interrogator, Tran. The tired, worn clichés echoed in his ears. Oh, how he wished he could be present when Tran learned he had escaped....

5
TRAN

HE HAD been handed over to Tran immediately upon arrival at the mountain camp. Pham untied his wrists and ankles, and led him toward the cluster of buildings. Four structures huddled close to the jungle wall—two long, low huts flanked on either side by smaller hooches.

The area before the huts was cleared, the earth packed down. One of the larger huts housed the prisoners. The second served as a combination mess hall for camp personnel and a classroom dedicated to the re-education of captives.

Six guards occupied one of the smaller huts. Hai Nguyen, the camp commander, and Dzung Tran, the political officer, lived by themselves in the remaining hooch.

Ramsey was to learn there were many similar holding camps scattered throughout the lower provinces of the North. Prisoners were processed and evaluated as to their potential propaganda value. Collaboration usually meant a move north, even perhaps to the Hanoi Hilton itself. Ramsey was never moved.

Pham had spoken rapidly to Tran, gesturing occasionally in Ramsey's direction. The younger man listened intently, staring all the while at Ramsey's battered face. Tran appeared to be remarkably nondescript, a stereotype, until Ramsey focused on his eyes. They were dark brown, almost black, searching, ranging inside Ramsey's skull.

He motioned Ramsey forward, until they were separated by no more than six inches. He continued to stare upward into the captive's eyes as if he were trying to gauge strengths and weaknesses.

He turned abruptly, indicating Ramsey should follow. Two guards fell in behind. He shuffled after Tran, barely able to negotiate the three steps to a wooden porch running the length of one of the larger buildings. The guards remained outside.

He entered the central room, which reminded him of a one-room schoolhouse. A large wooden table faced rows of benches. Other tables were pushed against the wall. At the opposite end of the hut an open doorway led to a cooking area. Posters depicting successful, happy workers decorated the otherwise austere walls. Behind the large table a portrait of Ho Chi Minh and a North Vietnamese flag were tacked to the wall.

Tran sat, indicating Ramsey should stand before the table. The interrogator selected a sheet of paper from a stack placed in a wire basket to his left. Carefully, with long, slender fingers, he arranged the paper in the center of a green blotter. As if he were taking part in some elaborate ceremony, Dzung Tran dipped an old-fashioned nibbed pen into a bottle of ink.

Finally he said, "Your name, if you please?" He spoke meticulous English, an indulgent smile played across his face. "John Ramsey," was the monotone reply. Tran waited, pen poised. Ramsey was going to make him ask, wait him out. He wasn't about to give a thing without effort. "Rank?" "Sergeant." Ramsey was enjoying the exchange. For the first time in days he began to feel alive, aggressive. "Serial number?" "1956658." Again silence. "Unit?" Up yours, buddy, that's all you get, thought Ramsey.

Tran carefully placed the pen aside, leaning back in the old wooden swivel chair. Elbows on its arms, he formed a pyramid with his hands, tapping fingers lightly against his lips. Again the eyes studied Ramsey intently. What they saw was a filthy, blood- and mud-spattered hulk. The man tilted to his left, concentrating his weight on the sound leg. His uniform hung in shreds. The lacerated wrists seeped blood that dripped from his fingers.

Tran returned his attention to the face. The lips were split and cracked, coagulated with blood. Ramsey's nose was swollen and puffy, an odd yellowish-blue color. But it was the eyes that worried Tran. The cold, blue eyes were not filmed over with defeat or resignation. They were the eyes of a pursued animal that had turned and chosen to fight.

Dzung Tran was an intelligent man. He had attended the university in Hanoi with a focus on history and government. But the ability to evaluate the behavior and motivation of his fellow man was the most valuable attribute he possessed.

This decrepit individual before him was going to be a challenge, perhaps the most demanding of his career. The task would be to break him, but not totally destroy. The man must remain a credible witness, not a vegetable.

"Sergeant Ramsey," he began, "I assume you to be a reasonably intelligent man. I am sure you can readily distinguish between fantasy and reality. Fantasy is a flight of dreams and imagination. The kind of flight you took in boot camp, listening to codes of behavior and conduct you were supposed to demonstrate when captured by a devious enemy. You probably conjured up images of yourself resisting honorably, never giving in to the myriad tortures of subhuman interrogators."

Tran paused, turning his gaze toward the open window, shaking his head slowly from side to side. His demeanor was that of an aged, erudite scholar. Ramsey was the impetuous romantic student unraveling the mysteries of the cosmos.

"It is not so, Ramsey. The words we live and breathe in the People's Liberation Army are, 'Prepare for the worst.' Are you ready for that? We Vietnamese have been fighting for thousands of years. We have never been defeated. Yes, we have lost battles and even wars. But, in the end, all foreign invaders have gone home.

"Did you know General Giap began his offensive in December of 1944 with thirty-four disciples? Now, in 1968, he commands an army of six hundred thousand. We have fought against the Chinese, Japanese, French, and now Americans, Koreans, and Australians. They too will go home, ashes of defeat in their mouth. Only we will remain, as we always have.

"You, Ramsey, will also remain, either as a corpse rotting in an unmarked grave or as a prisoner of war. How long do you think it will be before your people want their armies home? Five years, ten years, how long before it becomes apparent you cannot win?"

Tran scrutinized Ramsey's face, seeking a reaction to his predictions. Only the strain and agony of standing on the wounded leg were visible. The lips were pressed together in a thin pencil line. Sweat streaked his cheeks and neck, disappearing beneath the grimy collar of his uniform.

"So, Ramsey, how long can you survive? A month, a year, five years? Allow your mind to dwell on the question. You have only to make one simple decision. Cooperate, and you will live. Refuse, and you will die, vanishing from the face of the earth. That, Ramsey, is reality—cold, clear, factual reality."

Ramsey turned his face toward the window on his left. He felt very alone and vulnerable. Tran's words hung heavily, a foreshadowing of a long, dark tunnel with no respite from the gloom.

A line of men shuffled up the slope, crossed the trail, and halted in the cleared area before the huts. Ramsey was horrified by their appearance. Striped, pajama-type clothing hung loosely about their thin limbs. Their heads were shaved. Ramsey could clearly see oozing sores on skulls and feet. Despite exposure to the sun, the seven faces were gray and tinged with yellow. As he watched, arms were raised and two guards moved among them searching, probing the wasted bodies. Satisfied, the guards pushed and shoved the prisoners toward the other large hut screaming, *"Didi, didi!"*

"Well, Ramsey, that is what you will look like six months from now, and who knows in a year..." Tran left the supposition dangling and issued rapid commands to the waiting guards. "Before you leave, Sergeant Ramsey, let me inform you of our most important rule." Tran's expressionless eyes permitted a brief smile. "*Im lang,* do you know what that means, Ramsey?" No response. "I am sure you do, Sergeant. No talking. Silence, absolute silence. Should you choose to violate this rule, you will inhabit our cages. There you will have the privilege of becoming acquainted with our good friends, the river rats."

The guards dragged him from the room. He was barely conscious of his progress from one hut to the other. He sought to plant his feet and walk, but couldn't. His trailing feet made snail-like paths across the compound. Up the stairs, down a short corridor, and finally he was thrown into a narrow cell.

Ramsey huddled on the floor, gathering his strength. He was reluctant to open his eyes, afraid of what he might see. Finally he pushed his back against a wall, sat upright, and opened his eyes. Nothing, absolutely nothing, four walls of irregular cement blocks reaching to a flat wooden ceiling. No window, a heavy door with an opening six inches square, covered by wire mesh. Already he could feel the dampness of the earthen floor seep through his tattered fatigues. The cell was about six feet long and four feet wide.

He hooked fingers into the points of the cement blocks and pulled himself erect. He slid along the wall until he stood in a corner. Four and a half shuffling steps took him to the end of the wall by his right shoulder. Turning to his left, he moved two, almost three paces before he hit the far wall.

Ramsey turned, looking around his cell. From somewhere deep in his being he conjured up a dry, sardonic laugh. Shit! Shit! He giggled at the pure horror of his situation. All the manuals and all the instructors said the optimum time for escape was immediately following capture. How in the fuck could you possibly escape, strung like a fucking animal on a pole? Now Mr. Charles had stuck you in a cement hole. I really would like to meet those assholes shifting their butts behind comfortable desks who thought up the Code of Conduct for prisoners. Ramsey's mind flashed here and there sputtering with ideas.

There was movement in the corridor. The cell door opened. One of the hollow-eyed prisoners pushed a bowl forward across the threshold. "*Didi mau len,*" the guard behind yelled, dragging the man out of the cell door. The gray face managed to convey hope. As the door closed, thin fingers flashed a V sign. Then they were gone.

Ramsey sat, contemplating the half-filled bowl of liquid. Gratefully he tipped the contents into his mouth and hungry body. For some time he slept, propped against a wall. He had an hour or so of peace—no dreams, nothingness.

Doors were slamming, feet running, he heard "*Didi, didi*" again and again. A uniform, identical to that worn by the other captives, lay inside the door.

They came for him, grabbing, pulling him half-dressed into the corridor. Disoriented, and struggling to frame the surroundings, he found himself on one of the hard wooden benches before the table he had faced so many hours before.

Tran sat in the same position. The guards moved among the prisoners, slapping, kicking shins and feet, urging attention. Tran began, "Gentlemen, allow me to introduce the newest member of our little group. Sergeant Ramsey, would you stand, please." A rifle butt tapping on his spine suggested he comply with the request.

"Sergeant Ramsey was a member"—the emphasis deliberately heavy on the past tense—"of the Third Marine Division Recon Company operating from the combat base at Khe Sanh. He and other members of the group were spying on our movements along the Ho Chi Minh Trail. He was also trying to determine if our forces were building and poised to strike at Khe Sanh, committed to another Dienbienphu, as your General Westmoreland so greatly fears."

Ramsey was shocked listening to the extent of Tran's knowledge. "Unfortunately, we knew Sergeant Ramsey's team was in place. You Americans are, as we say, *Ngo,* stupid; our eyes and ears are everywhere. Sit down, Sergeant Ramsey, you are a poor excuse for a guerrilla. Captain Wilson, stand."

A prisoner in the front row of benches stood. The man's shoulders hunched over. He clasped bony hands behind his back. "Do you know what today is, Wilson? January twenty-fifth, your D.E.R.O.S. date. You Americans are so dedicated to that day. Your date of estimated return from overseas." He spat the phrase out, indicating disgust and sarcasm.

"Do you know it has been eight years, eight, since I left Than Hoa? That is why you can never win. Your one year in Vietnam is nothing. We are dedicated, totally committed to *Doc Lap,* independence. Your government would never fight a war for eight or ten years. You, Wilson," Tran's tirade continued, "what are you thinking? You should have been on your way home. Home to your wife and two sons, one of whom you have never even seen. Home to Corpus Christi, Texas. Don't believe it, Wilson, let the dream go. You will be swallowed up, as were all foreigners who have tried to invade my country. The jungle, the rains, the People's Liberation Army will defeat you. You will never see home again."

It seemed to Ramsey that Wilson had shrunk, folding in on himself with an involuntary shudder. Tran persisted. "Your only hope, Wilson, your last and final hope, is to cooperate. We are exchanging prisoners every day with the corrupt regime in Saigon. But you, Wilson, cannot be exchanged until you have proven yourself worthwhile, valuable. Sit down, sit down and contemplate your future."

It was growing dark in the room. Guards lit lanterns that sputtered, casting elongated shadows against the walls. Ramsey glanced sideways at his fellow prisoners. Uniformly they sat, hands draped between their legs, staring at the floor. How long before I become like that? he thought. His eyes started to close, a combination of despair and exhaustion suffused his body.

He snapped his eyes open, watching the little drama taking place. The other three men on his bench sat as before. Heads bowed, as Tran rambled to his captive audience. Each man, however, had extended the middle finger of his right hand. The men on the first bench had clasped their hands behind them, performing the same obscene gesture.

Ramsey's face wrinkled into a small smile. I am sorry, he thought. I misjudged you, I didn't think you were even alive. I will be one of you, I will resist no matter what they do to me.

"Ramsey," the voice penetrated his consciousness. "Tell us about your experiences during the past few months." Ramsey remained silent. "Come now, Sergeant, this is the one time during the day you are allowed to talk. Take advantage of this opportunity. Share your thoughts with the group. I am sure they are eager to hear the latest news from the front." Ramsey pushed himself erect, striving for some show of dignity. "What I would like to know, you ugly little fucker, is what you intend to do about my leg."

The guards closed in, fists and rifle butts drove him to the floor. They did not understand his words, but Tran's demented screaming goaded them on, urging retribution. As he was dragged from the room he heard the mocking voice. "Fool, you have so much to learn!"

He struggled pathetically, knees and feet bounced painfully down the steps. They were not taking him back to his cell. Finally the guards resorted to simply grasping his wrists and pulled him through the dust of the compound, across the rutted trail, and down the slope. At last they halted. Hands twisting his collar set the inert body in an upright position. He felt a hand spread across the middle of his back. He was propelled forward, through the open door of the cage. Face and chest smashed into the bamboo bars. Pain flashed to his dull brain, blood spattered from the twisted broken nose.

He grasped the bars and lowered himself to the floor of the cage. His head dropped between his knees and once again a deep, cold finger of isolation pervaded his being. At least in the hut there had been other humans. Human sounds, sweat, words, even emotions. Now nothing. Only he, alone in the night.

He extended his legs and pushed himself backward until he was able to rest against the bars sunk in the upper slope. He closed his eyes, trying to comprehend the events of the past few days and hours. He had been an alert, efficient fighting machine doing his time. Two short months left on the second tour. Going home; he had seen and done enough. What now? Here he was, a physical wreck, barely able to control his emotions. Tran was right, he was in some bad shit! But he'd been there before, right? Take the time on his first tour. He was a regular grunt. The missions were deadly and monotonous. Sweep and destroy, sweep and destroy. Take some hamlet with a number. Bust through, burn the hooches, kill the chickens, that was about it, except people died, mostly comrades. This one was different. He had bad vibes....

6

AN HOA BASIN

THE SLICKS had dropped the company someplace in the boonies. Where, no one knew. At least the L.Z. had been cold. The operation was as before: search the villes suspected of supporting V.C. activity in the area. Two days in the bush at most, hopefully. The first had gone as the manual predicted.

A nice day, just beginning, not too hot. They moved through the paddies and grass. The village sat, seemingly unconcerned. The villagers, of course, knew they were coming and chose to ignore that fact. If there were any V.C., they were long gone. It was almost a pleasant, pastoral scene. Old men and children leading water buffaloes down dikes between the rice fields.

First platoon waded complaining toward the ville, ignored by the inhabitants. Second platoon had divided, squads on either side setting in security. Smoke from cooking fires rose above the hooches. Welcome to another dawn on the wrong side of the world.

Ramsey, taking nothing for granted after ten months in country, moved his squad slowly, leapfrogging his fire teams. He knew any Charlies had bugged out, leaving the old ones and children to take all the shit and harassment. They always did.

The other squad leaders considered Ramsey a weirdo. He did not allow his people to mess with the population. You went into a ville and you knew they hated your being there. The air was heavy with it, sullen resentment. He could not blame them.

When he looked into their eyes he saw a world of hurt and resignation. Years and years of this sort of thing. He saw old, old eyes that said, "Why are you here? Why are you doing this to us? Why can't you leave us alone?"

So every time they went out he had a hassle. Some bad dude, believing he was a genuine killer, waiting, itching to waste a slope. He understood better when he had gone home between tours. Relatives, friends, all had the same question. "Did you kill anyone over there? How did it feel?"

Some guys had a need to kill, an absolute need to waste someone and take pictures of the body. He thought it had to do with being turned loose with the ability to administer the ultimate power of life and death. War permitted the evil in man to rise up out of the dark primordial depths and surface in the open.

He had absorbed the same old bullshit as everyone about kids being booby-trapped. Told never to trust any of them, you could never tell the enemy. Still, that didn't give you the right to wipe out the child population of Vietnam.

So he moved quickly with each team, pushing them, checking out the hooches. He could recognize by now the blood lust that rose in a grunt's eyes. That awesome feeling of power issued with an M-16. I have it, life or death. I can play God. Some of my buddies died in this cesspool of a country. I can burn you. I can rape you. I can stick a grenade up your ass and blow you away.

Ramsey methodically worked the teams through the ville. The other squads were firing hooches and cranking off rounds. His people looked as if they had been deprived and excluded from some precious ritual. Ramsey kept kicking ass. "Move. Move!" he screamed. "We don't need this shit!" He literally drove them into the brush at the far side of the village.

Boudreau, a long, tall new grunt from Cajun country, circled back toward the burning hooches. "Sit, man, sit, take it easy, don't do anythin' you're gonna be sorry for," ordered Ramsey. He made sure Boudreau heard his rifle click off safety.

"Ramsey, I'm gonna get you, you mother. First time we get a real firefight goin' you better watch your back." Boudreau flashed what he hoped was a treacherous smile to back up his threat.

Ramsey stared him down. "Boudreau, first time we have a firefight is when you're gonna see the death machine chew up people. You best have holes in the back of your skull, because I'll be bustin' caps every which way. You might stray into my field of fire."

They withdrew from the ville and humped for a distant ridge. The sun rose higher, the air superheated. Over the ridge and down into the waist of another valley toward the second village. They humped and complained. Nothing again, no contact. Ramsey's squad was left on trail security. The other squads moved through their positions sweating, cursing. The decimation of the hamlet began.

The captain called in security. This was grab-ass time. The troops let go rounds at some scrawny chickens running in circles. Smoke from the burning hooches drifted across the valley floor. The old people watched, eyes dull and accepting. Most of the grunts took some slack time, knowing there would be more humping to a night position.

Ramsey didn't like it; keep us moving, he silently urged the captain. They were hit. Heavy automatic fire from the tree line on the other side of the ville.

Two, three guys were down. Charlie started with rocket-propelled grenades, increasing the mad, screaming confusion. Michaels, Ramsey's platoon leader, only six weeks in country, was looking at him with large, pleading eyes.

"Tell the captain we'll try to flank them behind the paddy dike," yelled Ramsey. Reassured by some course of action, Michaels nodded vigorously. The captain lay on his back behind a small knoll screaming into the radio for a medevac and gunships. A runner delivered Michaels' message. A thumb hoisted in the air was his approval for the suggested action.

Ramsey got the squad moving. He ran weaving through the ville toward the small paddy. He could feel and hear the rounds snapping over and around him, over the dike and into the scummy water. The company was finally putting down some covering fire on the tree line. No one in the squad had been hit. They crouched waist deep, the dike rising three feet above their heads.

Some smart-ass machine gunner had picked them up and was spraying the top of the dike. Clumps of mud rained down. They moved, sinking lower into the liquid haven. Another seventy-five or a hundred yards and they would be level with the tree line.

Boudreau was on point, Ramsey directly behind. "Come on, bad ass, speed it up," goaded Ramsey. "I don't wanna grow old in this ditch. I'm gettin' too short to spend my time suckin' mud." Boudreau spun in a half circle. Ramsey raised his weapon, then saw the man's face convulsed with a hideous death mask.

The left side of Boudreau's jaw had vanished. Ramsey could actually see his smashed teeth and gums all the way back to the ear lobe. Ramsey caught him and jerked the shaking body down. "Sniper, sniper," he yelled back down the line of stumbling men.

Boudreau's eyes were glazing over, a pink bubbly froth escaping from the gaping hole where his mouth had been. The squad was down low in the water. Ramsey huddled behind the pointman's body, making himself very small. Another round punched into Boudreau's flak jacket. The body jerked, sending a fresh gout of blood spraying into the air.

The gunships came in, sweeping low over the ville, rockets and mini-guns hitting the tree line bathed in red smoke. Ramsey sprang to his feet, led the squad slipping and sliding, headed for the smoke. The sniper, like his buddies, had probably diddy-bopped, but you had to make the effort.

The gunships let up and rose in the air, hovering, providing cover for the medevac bird. The whole company was moving forward. Ramsey started the squad from their flanking position into the trees. Nothing, absolutely nothing; they had done their fade. The company came on, emerging from among the hooches. Ramsey's tactics had been perfect. The only trouble was the fuckin' stupid enemy refused to cooperate. Oh yeah! They had found a few blood trails and expended rounds. But nothing, nothing tangible, you couldn't vent your anger on a spot of blood.

This was how it happened. An atrocity in the making. Bewildered grunts with weapons, looking for something to kill. Old men, women, or children, it wouldn't have mattered. People you had lived with, suffered alongside, had their tickets punched, someone had to pay.

The medevac came in, dust whipping around the stony faces. It was this way many times. These guys believe all the bullshit, all the propaganda. They considered themselves the meanest, most bad-assed people walking the face of the earth. When some of their number got wasted they gave respect to Mr. Charles. It was a rationalization. Marine grunts had to take all the worst there was. They blamed luck, the Corps, the nebulous system that fucked them over, but never their tactics.

They had an aura about them, a fatalism that invited the spectre of death. The Air Cav was spoken of in disparaging terms—their caution, the precise movements of their operations. Marine grunts were born to hump. They scoffed at digging in deeply and constructing solid overhead cover. The basic attitude was put me one-on-one against Charlie, I'll be the lawnmower and his ass is grass. Unfortunately, the enemy chose not to fight the war as the grunts wanted.

Two medevacs were needed. Three troopers were

K.I.A., already zipped into green body bags. Five others on their way to Base Camp or maybe Japan.

Always, after a firefight, Ramsey's mind was blown. He was a bubbling cauldron of emotion. The pure rush, the exhilaration of being alive while others were dead. Pity for the casualties, but yet contempt because of their ineptitude. He felt aloof, removed, an observer. He knew he could survive on his own. The responsibility of the others weighed him down. The guys who believed they were invincible made mistakes. The ones who were so uptight, every move they made was a liability. Some of them smoked away each day, lost in a haze, until another date was crossed off on the calendar.

The company saddled up and moved slowly back down the trail. The adrenalin and fear generated by the contact were gone. They were dull, tired, one foot in front of the other, put 'em down, pick 'em up, the old routine of the grunt.

The night position had already been determined. A small knoll rising from the plain with a 360° perspective of the saw grass and paddies covering the valley floor. The hill surfaced like the hump of a whale above a sea of yellow and brown. It was an often utilized position, an old battle-scarred veteran in the mission's scheme of search and destroy.

The pace quickened, weary grunts anticipated some slack time before dark. A perimeter was set in, circling around the crest. They were able to use old holes and craters from previous occupations. Some were trash-filled, others had to be shoveled out and made secure.

Ramsey ignored the usual complaints, making sure each fighting hole was at least chest deep. "Come on, Ramsey," whined Trashman. "Enough is enough, this day's already a week long." Ramsey crouched low, staring into the perspiring face. "Trash, my man, when Charlie starts droppin' those big mortars around your ass, you'll wish you were a fuckin' mole. Now dig till all I can see is your eyeballs rollin' and clickin'."

He moved on, checking each squad position. They filled their empty sandbags; every man carried twelve. Parapets were built around each hole. The last precious hour before dark was spent cleaning weapons, eating, and smoking. A brief respite. A time of truce, both the hunter and the quarry standing down.

The word was passed, usual evening meeting at the C.P., platoon and squad leaders. The captain arrived at his normal pessimistic conclusions. "I just know we're gonna catch some shit tonight. S-2 is callin' a battalion-sized unit in the area. I figure they're gonna be sniffin' us out. I want fifty percent security at all times beginning at twenty hundred hours. The usual, no smokin', no talkin', no grab-ass. Let's have a listening post from each platoon. Three men down the slope off the trails."

The captain droned on, covering old ground. The same admission, again and again, the night belongs to Mr. Charles. They were the bait, dangling, waiting to be hit. Bust caps, inflict casualties, get the body count, medevac your own, move on, dig in, another day and then the night.

The briefing continued, the captain asking for mortar and machine gun positions. "Okay, that's it, we've got arty support from Base Camp and the gunships are on standby. We'll get illumination every fifteen minutes. That's all we can do." He sighed wearily, dismissing the group.

Ramsey, Lieutenant Michaels, and Thompson, the radioman, settled in behind the platoon line. Since Hendricks, the platoon sergeant, had been hit two weeks ago, Michaels had relied on Ramsey's bush knowledge. "What about the listening post, who do you think?" the lieutenant asked anxiously.

An easy grin slid across Ramsey's face. "How about you and the Skipper for the experience."

"Get serious, Ramsey, I'm still shittin' civilian chow."

Well, at least he knew his limitations. "That's a fact, Lieutenant, they'd smell your aftershave for sure. I'll give the lucky lads the good news," joshed Ramsey as he headed down to the holes.

He walked the line, eyeballing the positions. "Ah, there you are, Skater my man. Go get Mendoza and Boomer with the radio." The grunt stiffened visibly. "Ramsey, this ain't what I think it is, is it?" Skater blinked, shaking his mammoth head. Ever since PFC

James Weber had managed to milk a small shrapnel wound in his left buttock into two weeks in Da Nang, he had acquired the name Skater.

"Just givin' you the chance to show the world what a deadly, silent killer in the forest green you really are. Go get 'em!" Skater moved off, running his mouth to anyone who would listen.

Ramsey squatted, looking out over the darkening plain. Night was his favorite time. You were on the edge, waiting, but still it was beautiful. The sky all violets, orange, and dark blues. Later, in the deep dark, all the different sounds and hues of war to be absorbed, outgoing artillery, tracers, illumination flares, and now and then Spooky, the maximum killer, working an area.

It was like being a spectator at some awesome extravaganza, sending the blood pumping, exhilaration and fear all mingled and intertwined. The grunts returned, interrupting the ramblings of his mind.

"Cheerio, chaps, what we have here is rather a bully job." Ramsey often lapsed into an affected British accent that was intended to be humorous and hopefully relieved tension. "Cut the shit, Colonel Bogey," offered Boomer, a large lethal black from Philly, deadly with an M-79 grenade launcher. "Quite, Boomer. You know I'd much rather be going with you, over the top and all that. But alas, I'm needed here."

The three grunts looked at one another with total

disgust on their blackened faces. Ramsey got serious. "Okay, you know the skinny, down the slope, fifty yards. Stay away from the trails. Two men awake at all times. Key the set every half hour starting at twenty-thirty. The usual, one key, all quiet; two, contact, talk if you can."

The three half listened as they spread bug juice over exposed skin, hungrily sucking last cigarettes until first light. It was now almost totally dark. "That's it, go get some. After the first illumination round diddy on down there." Ramsey rose stiffly, massaging his knees, and headed to his hole.

Doc Waters had done a good job. The fighting hole had been deepened to Ramsey's specifications. The corpsman didn't have to do this grunt work, but he and Ramsey had become a team. It had been the sergeant who made him carry a rifle and ammo bandoleers. He had patiently explained how the V.C. loved to waste a corpsman. So he looked like a regular grunt, although the rifle was rusty and the bandoleer pouches carried field dressings.

Ramsey had developed a great deal of respect for Waters' cool under fire. The corpsman moved quickly, checking each casualty, ignoring the chaos swirling around, doing the best he could. That's all you could ask of a man in this sucking chest wound of a war. At times they talked far into the night, eclipsing for a few hours the horror and crudeness of Nam.

Waters sat now, wrapped in a poncho, spooning

fruit cocktail, a happy man. Ramsey spread out his poncho beside the huddled figure.

"Doc, you been holdin' out on me. Where'd you get the fruit? All I got left is ham and mothers."

"Well, I'll tell you, Ram, I was waitin' till some young aspiring Oriental done you in, but I couldn't hold out. Want some?"

Ramsey laughed. "Screw you, you probably haven't washed your hands since the last pecker check."

Their banter was easy and relaxed. "Doc, what's the word on the W.I.A.s? They make it?"

Waters shook his head in frustration. Government-issue glasses bounced on the bridge of an elongated nose. The thin, pale face with sad eyes turned. "Oh, fuck this place, Ramsey. Allen and Kendall were all over the place. Allen's gonna lose his leg and Kendall has probably checked out by now. His intestines were perforated with shrapnel. On the bright side, the other three dudes were lucky. They'll get to come back to this paradise vacation spot, maybe a month or so."

Ramsey caught real down vibrations from his buddy. When he was like this, he had to come around on his own. "I have to go check things out. Catch some peace and quiet, Doc, before the world goes mad." He touched the corpsman's shoulder as he passed.

It was early yet. Those on alert were active, animated. He slipped among the holes one by one. They acknowledged his presence in predictable ways. The new guys with excited, fearful whispers. "What d'ya think, we gonna get hit?" The veterans, cool, feigned indifference.

He caught a whiff of tobacco carried on the humid air. A shadow propped against one of the last remaining scrawny trees cupped a smoke in his helmet.

"Picarski, you dumb shit. I just got me a volunteer to walk point tomorrow. Douse it, asshole." The obscure figure hastily ground the butt and slid forward into a hole. There was a muted pop, the first flare burst over the valley floor. Swaying gently beneath the chute, intense white light sputtered and danced, throwing shadows across the grass and rectangular paddies. Like the lights coming on when the movie ends. You expect it, but still your eyes jump, trying to readjust.

Ramsey ran in a low crouch, dropping into a machine gun position. "What say, Burnsy, gonna get some tonight?" The startled gunner was clearly shaken. "Ramsey, don't do that to me. I'd like to tear you a new asshole. Just as soon a nice easy slide. Leavin' on R and R end of the week, remember? Gonna get some then, and they won't be wearing funny black pajamas."

"Shit, I bet after two days you'll beg to get back to your old buddies. Those babes in Hong Kong will eat you up." Ramsey tapped Burns's helmet and left the man to his fantasy.

Back at the hole Doc appeared to be asleep, or at least didn't want any conversation. Ramsey was restless; after the second illumination died he checked in at the C.P. position. "The L.P. report in yet, Lieutenant?"

"Yeah, all quiet." Michaels looked wiped.

"Crash for a while, Lieutenant, I'm wired up, can't sleep."

"Thanks, give me an hour or so."

Ramsey sat alone, back against the sandbags, the radio propped between his knees. A faint hiss of static issued from the handset dangling around his neck. He had been in country more than ten months, most of the time in the bush, playing boonie rat. He tried now, in his mind, to divide the time into events and segments of happenings. He couldn't; there was no nice linear beginning, middle, or end; it all ran together, his head filled with the sounds, smells, people, and emotions that were Nam.

Oppressive, heavy heat of midday sunbake in Arizona Valley. Freezing bone-grinding chill of nights in the highlands. The rain, always the rain and the red clinging, choking dust. Smells of decaying vegetation, cordite, and burning human defecation. The grunts he had come to know, the killers, the poets, the cowards and the braggarts. All their names and faces blending and flowing.

Then the people themselves, enduring, sullen, acquiescent. He had searched their faces time and again seeking an answer. In villes, flophouses, bars, and the resigned faces of occasional prisoners, he looked for an explanation. It wasn't there. Even the babysans with running sores and wide eyes echoed the same message. This is the way it has been and will always be. Don't expect your presence to make any difference. That's when he knew they could never win. Even if they sank the whole fuckin' country into the South China Sea he would still envision the old impassive faces with betel-nut-stained teeth.

The steady, hypnotizing hiss of static was broken by the handset's being keyed twice. Ramsey's mind snapped back, instantly alert. Depressing the button, he whispered, "Can you talk?" No transmission. "Stay low, hang on to your ass." He slid on his stomach down the slope to the neareast hole. "Contact mothers, time to earn your pay, pass the word." He reversed direction back to the C.P. "Michaels, shake it, man. Go find the captain. The shit is about to hit the fan. We got contact and they ain't friendlies. I'm callin' continuous illumination." Ramsey switched to battalion frequency and called the fire mission.

"What's comin' down?" The Skipper flopped alongside. Before he could answer, explosions ripped along the perimeter, immediately followed by heavy automatic rifle and machine gun fire. Both sides of the hill were being hit simultaneously. B-40 rounds thumped inside the lines. The grunts poured out return fire in all directions, firing LAAW and blooper rounds.

The night was filled with a crescendo of sound complemented by brilliant tongues of light flashing across the landscape. "Holy shit, Skipper, better get support in here most ricky-tick. We got us some bunch o' people out there." Ramsey had to yell in the captain's ear over the deafening roar of incoming and return fire.

Rolling down the slope he flopped into a hole, crashing into the hunched backs of the occupants. "What the fuck?" They collapsed in a heap. "It's me, Ramsey." They fought to untangle themselves. He recognized Jensen and Grenell. "For Christ's sake, don't scare us like that, Sarge. My asshole is still puckered."

The paddies and grass were bathed in white light, illumination had arrived. Ant figures were strung out across the landscape, coming over the dike and into the brush bordering the hill. In the far tree line, flashes of mortar tubes, an augur of destruction, only seconds away.

Ramsey was getting up, adrenalin flowing, pushing the fear back to an acceptable level. "Oh baby, Mr. Charles has come to fight. You guys see the L.P. come in yet?" He already knew the answer. They kept pumping out rounds, shaking their heads. An open sheaf of high-explosive artillery geysered across the paddy.

Screams of "Corpsman, corpsman" from a hole down the line. The mortars in the trees had them zeroed in now. Explosions ripped across the crest. Ramsey crawled out of the hole, heading back to the C.P. Halfway, he was lifted from the ground and slammed back down three or four feet away. Stunned and disoriented, he vaguely sensed shrapnel peppering his flak jacket and helmet. Lying on his back, gazing at the white revolving sky, he ran his hands tentatively over his body. Nothing. Then he discovered a warm, steady flow down his cheek and neck. Ramsey laughed, a nice clean slice, an easy purple heart.

Groping for his rifle, he dug elbows and knees into the hill, moving on up the incline. The C.P. had taken a mortar round. Foster, second platoon's lieutenant, was frantically trying to hold Michaels down. Blood was spurting with each heartbeat from the stump of his arm severed above the elbow. Michaels' eyes were rolling white, his lips pulled back, moaning and shrieking. "Mother of God, don't let me die. Please, please don't let me die." Doc scrambled up, stuck him with a morphine tube, and tied off the arm. Foster and Ramsey held him cradled in their arms until the frenetic eyes slowed and clouded over.

The captain was working the radio, a maniacal passion distorting his face. "Get me Spooky, get me fuckin' Spooky. We got an enemy battalion out there. You want meat, we got meat, come and get 'em." His face was scorched, the tattered uniform actually smoking. Both legs had taken shrapnel from the burst. He pushed Doc away. "Get lost, I'm okay. Take care of my troopers."

He continued screaming into the handset as if it gave a semblance of order to the chaos erupting around the hill. Doc was pleading with him, repeatedly tapping his shoulder. The captain brushed the offending hand away. Doc persisted. "Skipper, I gotta have some medevacs. We've got at least six priorities right now, including him." He jerked a thumb at Michaels, who appeared to be in shock.

"Can't be done, Doc, can't be done." The captain placed a fatherly hand on Waters' shoulder. "The birds couldn't get in here. They'd blow 'em out of the sky. You know it, and so do I. Do the best you can, Doc. That's all we ask."

Another round impacted, showering them with dirt. AK-47 rounds whipped overhead, pop, pop, their distinctive staccato rhythm whining through the eerie glow of smoke and diffused light.

They were in the grass now; the paddies were empty. Another white ball of light exploded on the perimeter. Screams, tracers burning down into the waving sea of grass.

Ramsey hunched down into his hole, watching the tree line for the next flash of a round on its way. Here it comes; he instinctively burrowed lower into the earth. The shell hit directly in front of a hole to his right. Sandbags, rifles, helmets spewed up into the night.

He talked to himself, "Oh yes, Charlie has his shit together; that's a one-twenty mm mortar out there. Spooky best get here soon or we are green sludge."

The grunts on the perimeter were rolling grenades down the slope. The L.P. had been given up for lost. A gray pall of smoke hung over the knoll, punctuated with red- and mustard-colored waves that drifted back and forth with each explosion.

Boomer came out of the saw grass. In the bizarre light he looked distorted and grotesque. His helmet and flak jacket were gone. He crawled up toward the line, every portion of the twisted body leaking blood.

Jensen slid up over the parapet of his hole. "Jensen, sit man sit, he's bait. They want us out there." Grenell hauled him back by the cartridge belt.

"Can't leave him, he's hurtin' bad," pleaded Jensen. "We gotta do something." Boomer was fifteen yards down the slope, inching forward. Low, moaning, guttural sounds.

"Keep comin', Boomer, go for it," Jensen screamed above the rolling thunder of exploding shells. His fingers dug into the slope, pulling him forward inches at a time. Boomer's body jerked and convulsed as he was hit again and again.

Jensen lobbed a smoke grenade beyond Boomer. Grenell and Jensen rolled forward, tumbling down the hill. Grabbing Boomer under the arms, they dragged the huge body back toward the line. Five yards to go, then vanished, swallowed by a gigantic flash of light.

The sappers came then through the holes blown in the perimeter. Once inside the lines, they used the confusion to cover their movements. Satchel charges destroyed a M-60 machine gun position, hurling the M-60 through the air like a child's toy.

From a hole near the C.P., Ramsey concentrated on the shadows slipping inside the perimeter. A stooped figure moved directly before him, zeroing in on the C.P. Ramsey cut loose, hitting the sapper in the chest and head. The man's legs kept going while the upper half of his body was propelled backward.

The other side of the perimeter had been breached. Regular troops were following up behind the sappers. The enemy was taking heavy casualties. The Marines concentrated firepower, trying to plug gaping holes in the line.

These tactics were new to Ramsey. They usually probed in small units, chopping you up piece by piece. Charlie wants us all, he thought, we're gonna be his example, stay out of my valley.

Dirt sprayed into his face. He swiveled in time to see a charging soldier. Ramsey burned off a whole magazine into him. The eyes went wide, surprised and pained, the body blown into a crumpled heap.

Off to the right the captain explained through gritted teeth, striving for patience, "We are being overrun. I repeat, overrun. Fire for effect, this position, immediately." There were many shadows, now working in teams, eliminating one hole at a time. Ramsey spotted two up on the crest outlined against swirling white smoke. He fired quickly, dropping one; the other slipped away.

Demonic screams rent the night. From behind, an AK-47 cut loose, smashing him forward against the earthen wall of the hole. An enormous throbbing line of pain ran across his back. Instinctively needing to survive, he twisted, facing the attacker. Five feet away, the enemy soldier raised his rifle, sighting in on Ramsey's head.

This was it, the end he had tried so hard to avoid. Ramsey knew he couldn't raise his weapon in time. He was frozen, resigned. A brilliant, flaming detonation shattered the soldier from behind. He was thrown forward into the hole. Ramsey collapsed, the body covering his own. The man's legs protruded up, exposed in the air. The upper body rested directly on Ramsey's chest. Dazed by the concussion, he lay confused and covered by his grisly companion.

Great chunks of the hill erupted. The barrage rolled across the crest. Guns from Base Camp continued to grind and pulverize the position. The company survivors burrowed deeper into the bottoms of their holes, earth and spent shrapnel raining down. Abruptly it ceased, ominous silence broken by moans, cries of the wounded and dying.

Then a new sound, a prolonged crescendo of fire.

Spooky had arrived and was working the tree line. Tracers curved lazily down, the Gatling guns saturating and shredding the area.

Dimly, Ramsey's ringing ears picked up the distinctive rattle of Spooky's guns. Then his mind registered the suffocating weight on his chest. The stench was horrendous, a mixture of sweat, excrement, and the sickly odor of blood. Ramsey's right arm refused to move. The flak vest had taken the shock of the rounds, but one had penetrated, high in the back of his arm. He arched his body up, pushing with the left arm. The corpse rolled to the side, diving headlong to the bottom of the hole. Blood, remnants of flesh clung to Ramsey's uniform.

He backed out of the hole and sat numbed, taking in the scene. It was reminiscent of the aftermath of a forest fire. The earth was actually smoking, a pall of gray hung over the entire hill. A moon-surface landscape, pockmarked and barren, ghostly figures fading in and out passed across his field of vision.

The C.P. was a bizarre scene caught in stop action. Radio clutched to his chest, the captain tried to suck in great drafts of air that bubbled and hissed, venting like steam, from a dozen holes in his body. Michaels was gone, a large bloodpool under his stiffening frame. Foster was immobile, head hung between his knees.

The whup, whup of rotors cut through the eerie silence. Some grunt with his shit together was using a strobe to guide them to the L.Z. on the crest.

Ramsey felt as if his brain and eyes were filled

with glue. Everything moved in slow motion. He had a thought of starting toward the choppers. But it took so much effort even to contemplate the action. He was so tired, floating effortlessly, lifting. A small jab in the arm did not make it to his brain. He drifted on a warm sea. . . .

7
CAGE TIME

THE LAUGH had a strange ring, a blending of dark humor and pain. Ramsey remembered that first night in the cage. He had carefully reconstructed the firefight. The wounding and the flesh of the enemy congealed on his uniform and hands. He conjured up every situation that had tested or threatened his courage. Whether in civilian or military life, he reviewed the tenacity that would not permit his quitting or giving up in any situation.

He had thought himself well prepared for captivity. It could not be any worse than all the pain and deprivation he had already been through.

Now, many months later, he sat and rocked back and forth like some asylum inmate. He spoke to the night and the yellow eyes outside the cage. "Well, fuck you people, I'm gonna make it. Two more weeks and I'm gone. Skyin' on down south to the land of the Big PX."

His thoughts again reverted to the first night. He had been half right in the assessment of his ability to function. The physical part was easy. Sure, his leg ached and his body constantly craved food, sex, warmth, everything associated with being free. He had been beaten, tortured, and deprived, but still he held himself together.

The danger lay in the mental part—they messed with your head. The isolation, the loneliness, the complete lack of communication with other rational human beings. Above all, the nagging suspicion lurking in the corners of the mind that the breaking point might be reached. Give in, cooperate, it would be so easy to let them have their way.

There had been times he had come close, right to the edge. But he had pulled back, retreating within himself, nurturing that part of self that was so precious. It had taken Tran long, long months to realize that politics, family, country, or physical abuse were not the paths to destruction of Ramsey's psyche. It had to be Ramsey himself; external forces did not control the man.

At the end of one particularly long and grueling session Tran thought progress had actually been achieved. The interrogator could not contain himself. "Well, Ramsey, you must admit it is an entirely stupid and senseless war. Primarily the reason for its continuance is the profits realized by your large corporations. Is this not so? The American people are unhappy with the war. Too many of their sons are dying or returning maimed and disfigured. All your tactics have failed—search and destroy, defoliation, pacification, denial of rice. Do I speak the truth?"

Ramsey nodded affirmatively. "You're right. So I tell you what. Get me a steak smothered with fried onions and a beer. I'll do anything you say." Tran's normally placid face contorted with rage. That little tête-à-tête had cost Ramsey a week in the cage. Thinking of it now, he laughed quietly.

Ramsey had more cage time than the whole camp put together. He knew the rats intimately and had given them names. The really negative aspect of cage time was simple: no sleep. If you succumbed to the sandman your little furry friends began to gnaw on your body. That's what he had been woefully unprepared for the first night. Images of the firefight and other Nam experiences had come and gone. He began to drift, release at last....

8
THE CAMP

THE FIRST sensation had been the claws digging into his thighs through the thin material of the prison uniform. Instantly awake, he went berserk, leaping up and smashing his head into the top of the cage. He lashed out, kicking and screaming until the cage was clear of their skittering bodies.

They regrouped outside on the riverside watching him, their yellow eyes unblinking. The rats had caught his scent far down by the river—blood and sweat mingled together. They had homed in on a potential meal. Ramsey's mind was blown, he shivered with revulsion and fear. He despised the rodents.

Throughout the night, whenever the man's head drooped and he became motionless, the animals made sorties around the cage. Given no alternative, Ramsey stayed awake, throwing handfuls of dirt at the heads peering between the bars.

Finally, as the first faint streaks of light spread across the sky, the rodents retreated. Creatures of darkness, they had no wish to see the light. The guards perhaps would make sport of them as targets, the prisoners possibly view them as an additional meal to supplement the vegetarian camp menu.

He dozed for perhaps an hour in the pre-dawn haze. He awoke startled by the sounds of the camp preparing for another day. A cart was drawn up on the trail. Two prisoners loaded tools and supplies. The remaining captives were scattered around the compound, eating. The hunched, pathetic figures were widely separated and monitored by two guards. Ramsey began to salivate. His stomach was growing smaller, but the mind sent a strident message, fill me, satisfy me to the limit.

At last one of the guards approached, followed by a prisoner carefully balancing a bowl. Ramsey immediately sensed a kinship. The man knew how important and precious the food was. He was trying his very best not to deprive Ramsey of a solitary drop. The gate opened, the man extended the bowl, a sly smile on his lips.

Ramsey took the proffered food gratefully. Cold cabbage soup, a minuscule piece of dark bread floating in the center of the dish. But it tasted like a gourmet delight. The cage door was left open as he ate. The guard who seemed to be in charge beckoned, pointing to the other prisoners falling into line behind the cart.

Greedily licking the last remaining drops from the bowl, he rose and ducked out of the cage. His whole body was cramped and stiff, but he welcomed the opportunity to move around, flexing bunched muscles and ligaments.

With a shrug of his shoulders and a questioning gesture using the bowl and spoon, he tried to communicate his confusion. What to do with the utensils? The guard impatiently indicated the line of prisoners, each five yards apart. "Keep it, man, keep it," the last man in line whispered hoarsely.

Ramsey fell in at the end of line. They shuffled on down the trail. He felt intensely stupid, a grown man stumbling down a road in North Vietnam carrying a bowl and spoon. He laughed, a deep gurgling sound dredged up from his gut.

The guard bringing up the rear of the column smacked him on the back of the head with an open palm. He could barely contain himself thinking of this ludicrous situation in which he had been chosen to play a part. Two guards rode up front in the cart, a line of zombies followed, going God knows where.

Well, Rams old boy, just keep your sense of humor and we'll make it through. The brief moment of levity passed, he limped along feeling the perspiration begin to flow. The sun climbed higher over the mountain crests. It was probably only about 0800, but already the heat was oppressive. Jesus, he thought, what's it gonna be like at noontime?

The column moved away from the river toward the interior. They struggled up the small trail, over a ridge, then descended into a lush green valley. The slopes on either side were terraced with paddies shimmering in the morning sun. To Ramsey the scene was tranquil, the war a distant happening.

National Geographic would love this, he thought, a perfect article, "Ingenious Use of the Land," that would be the title. The paddies were stacked one on top of the other all the way up the hills on either side of the valley. When the rains came the water could be regulated using the dikes, channeling the flow down to the bottom fields.

With reluctant admiration Ramsey surveyed the fertile valley. He concluded there was probably enough rice in this area to feed an N.V.A. regiment for quite some time. His fascination would fade in the ensuing days and months, dissipated by sweat and suffering under the relentless sun. The prisoners were slaves to this valley. Make new paddies where none had existed before, plant new shoots and harvest the ripened grain.

The column halted alongside a partially cleared area of brush. Ramsey followed the lead of the other captives. The line filed up behind the cart, each man to be issued a primitive tool of some type. He drew an ancient scythe with a long wooden handle and rusty blade.

The men formed a ragged line facing the remaining brush. He started forward with the others, guessing their task was simply to cut the stuff down to a level suitable for plowing. So it began; within twenty minutes the muscles of his body protested every swing. His leg throbbed, the backs of his thighs twitched involuntarily. Still, he was happy to be outside under the early-morning sun in the company of humans.

Every hour or so they would stop, retrace their steps, and pile the debris for burning. The guards sat behind the line of men. This, they knew, was easy duty. Their comrades to the south were preparing for the Tet offensive. They could relax and enjoy themselves, secure in the knowledge that their charges presented no threat of imminent destruction.

Guarding these hapless Americans presented no problems. They did not share the revolutionary zeal of Tran. All three were local militia and occasionally were able to receive their families at the camp. Ramsey was to learn that of all the guards, the one to fear was Oahn.

He was a brooding, humorless man, perhaps forty

to forty-five. He despised the Americans and took every opportunity to vent his hatred. Oahn's brother and son had died fighting these very same people he now guarded. He was ever watchful, his smoldering dark eyes seeking any infraction of the rules. When none was evident he would find cause to amuse himself with kicks or slaps.

The men on either side of Ramsey were five yards distant, seemingly engrossed in their work. With each swing, however, they exaggerated their head movements to observe the newcomer and check the guards' position.

On Ramsey's left was a tall, thin man with graying hair. A large, disfigured nose dominated his face. The pale blue eyes shot through with yellow flickered in a brief smile as Ramsey met his gaze. The mouth didn't seem to move, but the words were clear, "Take it easy, buddy, slow down. It's gonna be a long day." Ramsey whispered "Thanks," slowing his pace. Ten minutes passed in silence, the slow, rhythmic swing of their tools the only sound.

"What's your name, where you from?" Ramsey, thinking stateside, responded, "Ramsey, Boston." Again the prolonged wait. "Shit no, man, I mean here in Nam." Now he understood. "Khe Sanh. How long you been here?" The man was silent, bent to his task.

The guards had moved among the men, checking the progress. Oahn stared pointedly at Ramsey and his conspirator. "Move quickly, *chuyen nhank!*" he hissed, a menacing gesture of the M-1 rifle he carried enforcing the message.

The sun rose higher, burning off the mist lingering up on the mountainsides. Ramsey's sense of well-being evaporated like the mist as the heat of the day enveloped his body. As luck would have it, the smoke from the burning brush piles blew directly across the line of men. He was soon coated with dust, sweat, and sooty grime. He tried to wipe his watery eyes, but only caused further irritation. His throat felt filled with sawdust, lips caking and drying, finally sticking together.

He strove for a mechanical rhythm, dulling his mind to the exhaustion and pain. He slowly became aware the others had stopped. He drifted out of his robot trance and looked around. The prisoners had retrieved their bowls and sat patiently waiting. Two men brought a large pot from the cart.

The captives individually approached the container and filled their bowls, supervised by the scowling Oahn. He had the power to deny precious food. A prisoner's attitude or demeanor, any given whim, might cause Oahn to exercise this mandate and send a beaten captive shambling off choking back anger or tears. Also, he could dispense additional portions. Such domination over their very existence caused each man to advance with hesitancy and fear.

Ramsey reached the container. The guard lifted a hand, then slowly dropped it by his side. Ramsey was confused and apprehensive. What did it mean? He remained immobile, searching the guard's eyes for an answer. A voice whispered from behind, "He wants you to bow and thank him for the food." Ramsey hesitated, then bowed slightly. "Thank you for the food, you dried-up turd." Oahn frowned, not recognizing the additional words. He scrutinized the innocent face before him, then indicated the pot.

Ramsey filled his bowl and returned to his position. Seated, he chuckled—a little defeat, a little victory. It was impossible to determine the origin of the liquid. The taste was faintly reminiscent of pumpkin pie, but at least it was wet and fairly cool. His dehydrated body accepted the fluid gratefully.

The voice at his side spoke again, "Watch yourself with Oahn. He'd as soon waste you, no questions asked." The guards were gathered by the cart, eating. Every now and then Oahn would unexpectedly glance in the prisoners' direction, hoping to catch one in forbidden conversation. Ramsey repeated his earlier query, "How long you been here?"

"Name's Garrity, eight, nine months, it's hard to tell, every fuckin' day's the same." Garrity lapsed into silence, contemplating the landscape.

Surprise, surprise, a prisoner passed down the line handing each man a cigarette, extending a burning twig. Ramsey rarely smoked when he was in the bush, but anything to extend the rest period. The tube was short and strong. He immediately became dizzy and exploded into a series of harsh, dry coughs. Garrity laughed. "Nothin' like a good smoke after a hearty meal. Time to earn our keep."

The break was over. Work began again, accompanied by the shouts and taunting of the guards. The afternoon dragged unmercifully, a blur of heat and sweat. Ramsey forced his mind to other places, other times, shutting down the messages of agony moving toward his brain....

9
CATHY

BACK, BACK to Cathy, back to the Cape and a room facing the bay. They were so natural and easy with each other. A mutual acknowledgment that this time and place was right. No need for pretense or maneuvering. He saw clearly now as she stood across the room. She took a small delicate sip of her drink, placed it carefully on the dresser, and slid the straps of her suit down off the shoulders. Smiling innocently, she continued until the suit lay gathered around her ankles.

He too was now naked, absorbing the grace and contours of her body. Ramsey in his image creation tried to slow down the scenes, striving to remember and savor every movement and sensation. The figures behind his eyes seemed to move in exaggerated slow motion.

He crossed the room, cradled her face between his palms, and kissed the closed eyelids ever so gently. Still they did not fully touch. Her hands traced delicate paths down his chest, around his waist until they rested lightly, low on his buttocks. She pulled him close. Her nipples touched his chest and he throbbed against her pubic hair. Swaying gently against him, she brushed the hardened nipples back and forth across his body.

Ramsey probed her mouth and tongue as their movements became more urgent. He could feel the tightness and strength of her body as she strained against him. They separated and moved to the bed, arms encircling each other's waist.

He traced the shape of her body. Down her back, over her buttocks, the backs of the thighs. Then up, along the side of her legs, waist, and breasts to her face again, kissing the soft lips. He felt incredibly awed, it had never been like this before. A participation with his whole being in a mystical experience. He wanted to thank her, express his gratitude for the peace he felt....

10
OAHN

HIS VISION shattered abruptly. He was on his knees, driven there by a heavy blow between his shoulder blades. Oahn stood over him. The line of prisoners was ten yards in front of where he knelt. The remembrance of Cathy had been so poignant, so vivid, he had stopped working and stood frozen in the dream.

Oahn was screaming curses he did not understand. Ramsey laughed hysterically, fueling the guard's anger. He couldn't help himself, the mirth generated by the development of a large erection. It was an affirmation. Holy shit, he thought, I'm definitely still alive.

Struggling to his feet with a silly grin on his face, he bowed to the guard and rejoined the working party. He hurt, he was in pain, but the knowledge of what he had been able to do carried him through the last hours. I can leave this place any time I want. They may control my body, but my mind belongs to me and dreamtime.

Then came the small nagging thought that he might be going round the bend, off his tracks. He was pulling himself back to reality when he heard Garrity's whisper, "You okay, man?"

"Yeah, I was havin' some fun back there, forgot where I was."

"You know Morse code?" Ramsey nodded affirmative. "Try it on your cell wall, but be careful, there's a guard in the corridor all the time."

Finally the long, grueling day drew to a close. The prisoners, knowing instinctively, slowed and relaxed their pace. The guards called a halt, indicating they should load their tools. They sat gathered around the cart, preparing for the journey back to camp. The scene was tranquil, the valley a lush green. In the distance small children with their conical hats led plodding buffaloes home to the village. Along a paddy dike a motorcycle raised spirals of dust. Its harsh whining cut through the still air. Then it was gone, swallowed by the jungle, and the peace seemed even more profound.

The column began to move. Ramsey doubted he could make it back. His leg was numb, frozen, a useless appendage. He looked down, willing his foot forward. Take a step, take a step, he told the useless limb. The leg remained stiff and unmoving.

"Garrity!" he screamed. The guards and prisoners were stunned by this break in the routine. With infinite patience he explained, "Garrity, tell 'em my leg won't move. I can't do a fuckin' thing about it. Really." Garrity pantomimed, trying the explanation on Oahn.

The guard stepped behind Ramsey and jabbed his rifle barrel into the offending, quaking leg. Ramsey shuddered and hesitantly moved forward. He collapsed immediately, throwing hands forward to break his fall. A long stream of obscenities followed as he tried to push erect.

He was lifted and thrown into the rear of the cart amid tools and other equipment. Oahn climbed in alongside, kicking his inert form. The cold eyes studied him intently. Oahn sat with his knees drawn up, sandaled feet pressing into Ramsey's side. For a time Ramsey returned his stare, then gave up and closed his eyes. The jolting, rocking motion of the cart lulled him into a light sleep.

He woke to the insistent prodding of Oahn's feet exploring his rib cage. Some feeling had returned to the leg. He slid over the end of the cart and with slow, measured steps joined the other prisoners lined up before a rusty pump in the corner of the compound.

Each man was allowed ten seconds at the pump. Eating utensils were scoured, and, briefly, the man himself, before being led off to the cell block. Ramsey knelt in the mud and worked the handle, allowing the cool water to cascade over his head. His lips worked frantically, sucking in the moisture as it flowed past his mouth. The guard tapped him lightly with his rifle.

Back in the cell, he regarded with some amusement the slop can covered by a wooden board. I can't even remember the last time I took a crap, he thought. He surveyed the cell, wondering how he should occupy himself. This was supposed to be quiet time before the evening meal.

He recalled Garrity's question about Morse code. Searching the damp earth, he located a small pebble. He retreated to the corner nearest the door where a small portion of the outside corridor was visible. Ramsey tapped, "Hello." Nothing, silence. He tried again. No response. The echo of his tapping hung in the air.

Footsteps approached his cell. Dropping the pebble and covering it with his foot, he shrank into the corner. The door opened. A guard beckoned to him, indicating out. Shit, he thought, the cage again or even worse. The guard, however, did not seem angry or aggressive.

He was pushed to the far end of the narrow passageway. The guard stepped around him and opened a door. Ramsey, fearing the worst, peered inside. It was the basic supply room. Pallets, blankets, and clothes occupied half the small room. The other side was piled high with cut yellow saw grass.

The guard made scooping motions and pointed at the grass. Ramsey understood; this was material for his bed. He carried armfuls back to the cell, spreading and covering the dirt floor at the far end opposite the door. Back to the supply room, the guard, holding up two fingers, pointed to the blankets. They were thin and moldy, but what the hell, mused Ramsey, there's no place like home.

He spread one of the blankets on top of the grass and lay down. Sharp stalks dug into his body through the threadbare material. His last thought was, Economical little bastards, and he drifted off into oblivion.

Sounds of activity in the corridor awoke him. The cell door opened. A prisoner, accompanied by the inevitable guard, delivered the evening meal, a rice ball surrounded by pumpkin soup and hard brown bread.

Ramsey addressed the walls, "Perfect, a little late-afternoon siesta, awake to a fine meal, what more could anyone ask?" He ate slowly, prolonging the ecstasy. He decided to save half the bread for later in the night and secreted the remainder beneath his blanket.

All too soon the guards arrived. As on the previous evening, they were herded toward the main building. They shuffled into the room and there was

Tran, poised, waiting to deliver his nightly diatribe. He seemed particularly buoyant and animated. The room was cool and dank.

The gray men took their places on the wooden benches. Ramsey was barely functioning, totally spent from the long, draining day. He slouched forward, arms hanging between his knees.

Tran surveyed the room, pleased with the assemblage of his star pupils. "Good evening, gentlemen. I do hope you have had a productive day. Let me remind you once again, I am not an interrogator, but a teacher. Once you have been re-educated and cooperate with the People's Republic you may return home. It is a simple as that, an elementary question of understanding."

Tran then launched into a history of Vietnam from the Communist point of view. Every negative aspect of history was, of course, attributed to foreign influences. Each positive advancement was attributed to the Communist regime.

Ramsey's attention lagged and his heavy eyes fluttered. The guards posted around the room made their presence felt. It would be impolite to interrupt Tran's monologue by waking inattentive prisoners, so they were particularly noisy. They shuffled constantly, scraping boots and inadvertently banging rifle butts on the wooden floor. Only Oahn moved among the prisoners, prodding viciously, not for Tran's sake but for his own satisfaction.

Tran was winding down. "Finally, I will have some concrete news for you in the next few days. There are great movements taking place that will convince your government we are totally dedicated to your destruction. Your war is lost. I implore you, cooperate now before it is too late and you are swallowed up by the aftermath. Return now to your cells and consider what I have said. All is lost. When we win, you will vanish like chaff in the wind. Sergeant Ramsey, you will remain behind, please."

The other prisoners left the hut rapidly, escorted by the guards. His being went with them, knowing they were destined for at least some peace and quiet. Ramsey focused his eyes on the sputtering lantern behind Tran. Come on, man, I have to sleep, he thought. The trembling legs betrayed what it was costing him to stay erect.

Tran was like a well-fed, satisfied cat. Leaning back in the swivel chair, he smiled at the disheveled, desperate man swaying back and forth before the table. He chose to extend the silence, pleased with Ramsey's obvious torment. Time plodded on, insects flitted around the flickering light, occasionally self-destructing against the hot glass. The only other sound in the hut was the hypnotic creaking of the chair shifting from side to side.

He finally spoke, the tone of his voice soft and mellow. "Well, how was your first day in our little community?" Ramsey was instantly alert. This guy wants to hear all my troubles. No way! "Not too bad," Ramsey answered. "I mean, given my choice there's other vacation spots I'd rather visit. The food leaves a little something to be desired. You people must be really hurting if that's the best you can do."

The chair banged forward. Tran's dark eyes flashed with anger. "Ramsey, the lack of food is a direct result of your government's campaign to destroy our rice crop with chemicals and aviation fuel." Well, I have to go along with that one, thought Ramsey. He had seen a group of villagers who, while carefully planting new rice shoots, had been doused with gasoline from a chopper crisscrossing the paddies. They had screamed and raised their futile curses toward the bird.

Tran regained his composure. "As I stated previously, Sergeant Ramsey, I am not an interrogator, but a teacher. In this role it is my duty to hasten your re-education. You will not be tortured or beaten as you probably expected. Instead, you will be enlightened concerning the plight of the oppressed peoples around the world. Once you have accepted our teaching you will go home to spread our message."

Ramsey suspected he would be hearing this line many times in the coming months. He had never heard of any repatriated prisoners or, for that matter, any escapees. Still, the word "home" sounded magical, however implausible the promise.

"In addition, Sergeant, once you have begun to cooperate you will be granted numerous privileges that will ensure your survival. You will receive more food, careful medical attention, and will be excused from the field details."

The last promise clicked in Ramsey's mind. There had been fewer men in the fields than had assembled for the evening meetings. So, they were collaborators. Men who had been driven to the brink and in a last desperate chance for self-preservation had let the flame die.

Tran continued, but Ramsey's thoughts dwelt on the nameless, faceless men. He made a silent promise to himself. He would never, if humanly possible, give in. But he would not or could not condemn their weakness, their need to survive. He felt pity, not anger. What had been done to them? What would make a man turn against himself and all he believed?

Tran's anger broke through his speculation. "I sense you are not paying attention. Do you wish to occupy the same accommodations you were assigned last evening?" He had Ramsey's total attention. "I understand you had some difficulty completing the work today. Sad to say, Sergeant, you may not last very long in your condition. We work every day. It is necessary, there are no days of rest. The People's Army must be fed. The choice is yours. We ask only that you sign a statement and make a recording. Such a small thing to save your life. Is that not true?" Ramsey said nothing. "No matter, we are in no hurry. Time is all you have."

Tran dismissed him, an indifferent wave of the

hand. Ramsey shuffled from the hut exhausted and befuddled. A guard waited on the porch and escorted him across the compound to his cell. The thought of making contact with the prisoners on either side was too much. His mind tried to focus on the day's events. Protective body mechanisms were closing down, counseling sleep, sleep. He drifted off into neutral space where there was no pain, no hunger, simply quiet....

11
COLLABORATORS AND SCAVENGERS

NOW THE dawn of another day, many months later. But still it would be the same, an endless parade of repetitious days. Only now he had hope. The time of deliverance was approaching. This burning, flickering light would carry him through. There would be the work details. There would be Tran's relentless orations. Still, with this precious secret he could endure the long, measured procession of time.

The sun flamed above the ridges, illuminating a face contorted into a secretive guise. His movements were furtive. He patted and smoothed the earth of the cage floor. The red eyes darted from side to side.

Since his decision to escape had been made, Ramsey had become obsessed with the need to nourish his remaining strength. He carefully plotted each move, questioning every action, evaluating the energy to be expended. He stole, scavenged, and foraged for extra food whenever possible. Anything at all was a potential source of nourishment. Roots, berries, and even insects came under his scrutiny. He emulated a wild forest creature preparing for the winter.

On work details he labored as slowly as possible without drawing attention to himself. His manner became servile, cultivating the image of a model prisoner. He avoided any word or activity that might provoke an angry response from his captors.

When he desired the solitude of cage confinement to think and plan, the offense had to be carefully orchestrated. Just enough of a violation, but not too much that a severe beating might follow. The guards were unpredictable, their particular mood at the time dictating the punishment administered. Ramsey avoided them, preferring to aggravate Tran, whose response could be anticipated.

In all the days of captivity he had never seen Tran physically abuse a prisoner. Perhaps he sincerely thought of himself as a teacher rather than an interrogator. The retribution for erroneous behavior or thinking was uniform. Tran provided the solitude of the cages, urging the captive to meditate upon his misdeeds.

The morning meal was delivered as usual, by a prisoner with guard in tow. Ramsey ate slowly, as if the length of time spent chewing and savoring the food was in direct proportion to the nutrition he derived from the meager portion. The men began to assemble for the daily work detail.

Only three original faces were familiar from his early days. Garrity was there, resilient as ever. Swanson, who had arrived a month after his own capture, stumbled into line. Most surprising of all was Wilson, who by all rules of the game should have broken. He had remained impervious to all the promises of contact with his family. Ramsey felt deep and open admiration for him.

Every month a truck would arrive at the camp. The prisoners who had shown the slightest inclination toward collaboration were shipped out, moved on, farther to the north. On the morning of the truck's arrival all prisoners ate in the large hut rather than in their cells. Those who were departing received a substantial breakfast of eggs, rice, and some unidentifiable meat. In addition, letters and packages that had been held back were distributed.

The room was electric, unexpressed emotion ricocheted off the crude walls—collaborators, eager to devour precious letters but ashamed of the price they had paid; those remaining behind aloof, resentful, but coveting the tangible representation of the life they once knew. Letters were hidden, secreted away from hostile, vicious eyes. Low, animal-growling sounds were suppressed by vigilant guards.

The camp commander began his standard speech, dutifully translated by Tran. He assured those remaining behind that to cooperate was in their best interest. He urged they follow the footsteps of those who were leaving, the only road to survival.

These little turds surely know how to yank us around, thought Ramsey. I am never taking that ride, he vowed, joining the others forming in line on the trail. It's too late. I'm gonna beat them. I'm long gone. The idea would carry him through another day.

The early-morning air was cool and pleasant. Heat waves would later shimmer, oppressively rising up from the valley floors. They walked slowly behind the cart, absorbing the myriad lush green colors of the jungle pressing in on either side.

Ramsey's eyes roamed, searching along the trail for any edible morsel. The trail guard was new, an enigma in that he smiled a great deal. Ramsey had labeled him Dopey. He functioned in a world of his own that did not include the grotesque events of each day. His weapon slung carelessly over his shoulder, the guard strolled along, oblivious to the reality of the situation.

Ramsey spotted some wild yams bordering the track. He quickly scuttled into the brush and snapped two of the long tubers from a plant. Dopey watched, a vacant expression on his face. The flesh of the plant was moist and filling. Back in line, Ramsey offered hunks of meat to the guard. He accepted, bobbing his head in gratitude. "Dopey, I sure as hell hope you're on duty when my time comes," Ramsey smiled, patting him gently on the shoulder.

Today they would be planting new, tender shoots of rice. It was back-breaking work, stooped all day in the paddy. At least when they were clearing brush it was in an upright position and the energy of swings could be faked. It was much easier for the guards to spot inactivity while planting.

Some of the prisoners worked on their knees, partly submerged in the low water. Ramsey was an advocate of this method, working with his back to the guards. Holding his basket before him, he ate about every tenth plant. He paid later on at night. Squatting over the slop bucket, cramps gripping his intestines, he dripped thin, vile-smelling fluid into the container. But he figured what the hell, the plants provided some nourishment.

The prisoners made a concentrated effort to sabotage their work. The delicate shoots were mutilated, root systems destroyed. An elaborate warning device had been developed to alert captives at the approach of danger. A series of coughs or water splashes indicated the presence of a guard or his interest in a particular man.

As he worked, Ramsey watched carefully for any sign that it was getting close to the noon meal: the prisoners who received their portions first had a better chance at the chunks of vegetable floating in the thin fluid. Also, they had the opportunity to finish first. If anything was left in the pot, the guards usually allowed the prisoners to help themselves.

Lately, Ramsey had always managed to be close to the food at the break. He had no guilt feelings at all about the scheming and conniving. It was in his mind a pure, simple struggle to come through intact.

It was time; the guard lifted the canister from the rear of the cart. Ramsey straightened his aching limbs and hobbled rapidly toward the dike bordering the rice paddy. The other prisoners, taking his cue, stopped work. They, of course, had observed his behavior and dismissed him as another one slowly going down the path of insanity.

First in line, his bowl was filled with potato soup. He did not bother to sit, but quickly swallowed and rejoined the line after the last man. In his mind he associated filling his body with food with the successful completion of his escape. The more he ate, the stronger and more capable he felt. He drank the second bowl slowly, congratulating himself, pleased with his resourcefulness.

Swanson, to his right five feet away, examined him carefully. "Hey, man, you gone dinky dau?" Ramsey uttered a low, hysterical giggle and tipped his bowl. "Say good-by, mother, I'm short in this place." He squatted, Asian style, staring straight ahead. Swanson checked him out, still not comprehending what he had heard. "You're one crazy son of a bitch, brother, you know that?"

"Yeah, I know, but you got any better ideas?" Ramsey's smiling countenance didn't change. Swanson breathed deeply. "Fuck no, man. How you gonna do it?"

The guards were starting to stir, making signs of getting back to work. "Stick close, I'll try to fill you in, maybe even drag your black ass with me."

Back in the paddy, Swanson edged as close as he dared without creating suspicion. "Come, asshole, give," he whispered. Ramsey grinned. "I'm goin' down that big old river to the sea. After that I don't know, steal a boat maybe."

It was Swanson's turn to laugh. "Shit, great. I can't swim. Never been in the ocean in my whole life. That would be somethin', a dried-up black prune makes his escape. You're on your own, buddy. Need any help, lemme know. Otherwise forget it."

The guards were moving around now. Time to quiet down. The afternoon was routine—long, hot, and miserable. They moved as ghosts, sifting through the undulating heat waves. Even the guards were quiet and restrained under the blanket of humidity and the burning furnace of the sun.

Then it came, a familiar yet almost alien sound to their shrunken world. The beat of a chopper far to the southeast floated over the paddy. The men stopped, raising their eyes to the distant rhythm. It was a forlorn, haunting call, a clarion of freedom. The rotors were throwing out threads, pulling them in, away from this stupid, obscene place. The beat faded. And with it their dreams.

The remaining time of work found each man subdued, closeted with his own thoughts. The return march was silent and plodding. They submitted passively to the evening search, retiring sullenly to their cells.

Ramsey had one more night to serve in the cage. He checked into the enclosure, accepting the small area as his space, his given home. Now was sleep time, before full darkness. Now he could gather himself, recover from the long day's ordeal. Later, in the middle of night, he would plan, rehearse, and live his escape.

The mountains circling the camp took on countless shades of green. The dying sun filtered down through passes, reflecting off the jungle canopy. Ramsey settled into a corner, back against the bars, and closed his eyes. He drifted into dreamless sleep.

Sometime later he awakened. The cage door was open and the evening meal had been delivered. The air was cool. The sun had slid behind the ridges. Ramsey changed position, turning to face the camp. Oahn was seated on the porch of the main building, weapon across his thighs. This was the Number One guard's position. Number Two's was a chair at the head of the corridor in the prisoner's hut. The third guard was relief.

Even in the monsoon a guard would be stationed on the porch. The sheets of rain would obscure his movements. But still, maybe he needed a diversion while he dug his way out. He would ask Swanson. He would know what to do.

Oahn was fifty yards away, but his eyes appeared to be focused totally on the cage. Ramsey knew the guard's secret desire was to reduce him to a sniveling, crawling wreck. Vibrations of hatred emanated from his body in Ramsey's presence.

On one particular occasion Oahn had almost achieved his wish. Tran was inspired, delivering an emotional political speech, building to a climax. He could hardly contain himself, enumerating the numerous victories of the Tet offensive. Finally he concluded with the prediction that the great Marine firebase at Khe Sanh was within twenty-four hours of total collapse.

Ramsey voiced his unsolicited opinion: "Bullshit, total crap." He was lifted from the bench by the collar and thrown to the floor. A rifle butt pounded into his ribs and stomach. He lashed out wildly and Oahn sprawled on top, punching and kicking. Another guard jumped on his chest. Ramsey's flailing arms were pinned to the floor. Oahn grasped his wrist, spreading the hand and fingers. A steel butt plate smashed repeatedly, grinding his bones into the grimy planks.

"Enough, enough," ordered Tran. Ramsey lay curled and moaning, cradling his battered hand. Oahn stood over him panting, eyes blinking rapidly, eager for more. "Sergeant Ramsey, your attitude is extremely poor. For this you must be punished. You are not only disturbing me, but also your own comrades," admonished Tran. Another spell with the river rats.

Such incidents were occurring with increasing regularity. So much so that Ramsey had decided he must go soon, before the guard achieved his final revenge.

Only a week previously Oahn had come upon him silently while he nibbled on some scavenged tidbits. Oahn kicked him forward into the mud and water. Ramsey struggled helplessly while the guard stood on his back. His head was forced deeper into the mud. He panicked, sucking in slimy water and human waste. He was filled with rage and terror. He twisted and thrashed. One last desperate heave relieved the weight on his body.

He rose to his knees, choking and clawing the mud from his nose and mouth. When he finally filled his lungs, the curses poured out. "You lousy, fuckin' dink bastard. You rotten piece of slime. I'll get you, I'll get you."

Oahn stood over the pathetic, kneeling figure. The guard swung his weapon slowly till the muzzle rested directly under Ramsey's chin. Ramsey trembled, clenching his fists in an effort to control the building fury. He looked up into the sneering face. The guard exerted upward pressure with the rifle, forcing Ramsey to stand. The taunting eyes never left the prisoner's face. He's just aching for me to make a move, thought Ramsey. The miserable little shit would get his rocks off squeezin' out a round. The two enemies stood motionless until finally Oahn ended the confrontation with a simple "Work!"

Ramsey closed his eyes, shutting out the dim figure seated on the porch. He slept until his sensory warning system picked up the approach of intruders. "Hey, men, how goes it tonight?" In the muted light cast by a sliver of moon he could distinguish the rats reconnoitering the cage area.

Sniffing and scratching, they sought any scrap of edible material. Now and then one of the bolder rodents would try to squeeze between the bars. Ramsey would go into action, cursing and scooping handfuls of earth at the invader. Occasionally he would unearth the secreted digging stick as a last resort. After scouring the area clean the rats drew back, but still remained within the range of his scent.

Despite the conditions, he felt rather mellow and

peaceful. There would be two or three hours of think or dream time before the dawn, a signal for his next sleep period. The rats would be gone, retreating before the sun.

His only regret was lack of communication.

12
COMMUNICATION

IN DEFIANCE of the silence enforced by their captors, the prisoners were able to relay an enormous amount of information. Usually, incidents of punishment were related to breaking the silence rule. The guard stationed in the cell corridor was supposed to prohibit any noise. Still, the captives were able to employ their tap code.

Swanson had taken it upon himself to keep the information flowing. He and the others tapped furiously on the cement blocks. All types of messages filtered along the row of cells. Personal information, the latest battle-scoop from new arrivals, personal thoughts, and even prayers were shared in their little community.

It was such a sensitive network that even attitudes and emotions could often be determined between senders and receivers. There were at present eight men at the camp, two officers, six enlisted. The prisoners reflected different levels of education, age, and commitment to resist.

Always an indication that a prisoner was wavering or shaky was a breakdown in communication. Swanson or Ramsey, as the hard-core leaders, would frantically try to rally the despondent man to rejoin the fold. Once communication ceased altogether, the man was gone and would probably be on the next trip north.

Ramsey had learned to interpret and gauge a sender's mood by the subtle nuances hidden in the content of his message. Of the eight men in captivity, five were solid, two were fluctuating, and one had collaborated. Neither Ramsey nor Swanson passed judgment. Their main goal was unity, believing if they all hung together survival was possible.

The older and more experienced prisoners tended to perceive the situation more realistically. Other contributing factors were intelligence and education. The younger, more naive captives, not yet sure in their own concepts of self, had difficulty looking beyond the present reality. The result of this preoccupation was self-pity.

Every new prisoner went through this initial stage. The typical reaction was, why me, why me? This was also a time of counting losses. A time of aloneness, sitting in darkness, crying silently.

Most men were able to shake this despondency. Each man had his own device—imagination, logic, anger, pride—whatever it took to make the decision for survival on his terms, not the enemy's.

Ramsey recalled some who could not save themselves. Bates was one. Ramsey knew very little about the man. From the beginning, he refused to respond. Weeping could be heard nightly from his cell. Swanson had gone nuts in the adjoining room. He had beaten on the wall and finally started to scream at the silence. "For Christ's sake, man, you got help here. There's hope, talk to us!" The guards took Swanson away. Bates was gone within a week.

The one they had hated to lose was Davidson. He arrived about four months after Ramsey. A stocky, feisty little soldier, he had immediately joined the network. A natural-born rebel, he had attempted to escape shortly after being captured. Local militia had cornered him and administered a severe beating.

Davidson was a door gunner, the only survivor, thrown from the burning wreckage when his bird went down on the wrong side of the DMZ. Between the crash and his treatment by the locals, he was a mess. They brought him into camp on a crude stretcher.

Even though Davidson was barely conscious, Tran had immediately tried to interrogate him. He promised expert medical attention in return for cooperation. Davidson's reply had questioned Tran's ancestry, his manhood, and the status of his mother. In spite of his condition, he was deposited comatose in the cage.

Ramsey and Swanson became his protectors. They took chances to whisper words of encouragement and scrounge extra food to sustain the decimated body. Davidson survived. He eagerly mastered the code, becoming one of the more ardent communicators.

They had to shut him up until he was given necessary survival information. Within the first two weeks Davidson knew what to expect during the interrogation sessions. He learned the tactics Tran would utilize, which guards to avoid, and the limits of his own conduct. Once such information was passed along they turned him loose.

Davidson wanted to know everything and ignored Swanson's warning to slow it down. He was back again, tapping like crazy. He supplied knowledge of Westmoreland's departure and the assassination of Martin Luther King. Why Tran had held back this particular information neither Ramsey nor Swanson could figure.

Davidson was a small-town boy from the Midwest.

He had married his high school sweetheart shortly after graduation. Both sets of parents objected, but the young lovers were adamant. They were deeply in love, so much so that Suzanne, his new wife, supported his decision to enlist.

Her letters had been filled with hopes and plans. Almost eleven months of his tour were gone before he was captured. Naturally, no more letters. Davidson knew rationally they were still coming and were waiting someplace. But the absence of the letters slowly deflated his normally buoyant spirit.

All of this Ramsey and Swanson knew. Whenever Davidson's communication faltered, they understood he was thinking of Suzanne and her letters. They would quickly respond with humorous anecdotes, drawing him out of his downer. Eight weeks after his arrival Davidson suddenly went silent. At night they heard nothing; during the work details he moved like a zombie. He would neither look at them nor respond to any attempt at contact.

They could see he was deeply troubled but could not break through the shell he had built. Ramsey noticed his meals were unfinished or even ignored altogether. A guard had beaten Davidson on a work detail because he seemed to refuse an order. It appeared as if the man was completely oblivious to the blows. The others took turns communicating for hours at a time every night, risking discovery.

At last he broke. A soft, tentative message coming

through the walls. The entire story poured out with what Ramsey interpreted to be a combination of anger and sadness.

At the conclusion of a session with Tran, the interrogator, as he left, casually offered congratulations on the birth of a daughter. Davidson was numb, unable to orient his thoughts. A jumble of questions ran through his stunned brain. The guard had to lead the slack-jawed prisoner back to his cell.

He curled in a ball on the cold floor. Points of light danced inside the tightly closed eyes. It's not possible, a silent scream. What the fuck is goin' on? Tran's lying, he's tryin' to rattle me. He spent a torturous, sleepless night ignoring the messages and questions tapped on his wall.

His stomach constricted in knots. He lay on the blanket, emotions running ragged. He would sweep away Tran's words, only to have them creep back into his mind.

Davidson had not seen his wife for almost thirteen months. Now she was the mother of a child. Whose child, whose child? She had not been pregnant when he left. They had taken precautions against the possibility of his death. If something had gone wrong, she would have written. No, no, I believe in her, he vowed. The thoughts tumbled and reeled in his head.

In the morning he had requested permission to see Tran. The interrogator had refused to see him until the next session. For the next five days he was a man demented. He knew it couldn't be true. He knew it was a strategy.

Still, thirteen months was a long time. Suzanne was a sexy lady, thoroughly enjoying their sexual encounters. He had himself been tempted several times since leaving home. She wouldn't, she couldn't. It's a trick, damn it, a fuckin' lousy dink trick.

He stumbled through the days, exhausted by the sleepless nights. The others couldn't penetrate the fog of doubt enveloping his mind. At last he was taken to see Tran. Davidson's agitated demands for answers were dismissed by Tran as trivial to their conversation. He did, however, agree to discuss the questions, if there was time, at the conclusion of their meeting. The war and its ramifications would occupy the majority of their time together.

Davidson's concentration was shot. He could not recall later what had been asked or how he responded. He was vaguely aware of providing information to satisfy Tran's insistent probings and hurry the end of the session.

The interrogator appeared satisfied and dismissed him with the typical casual hand movement. Davidson begged, reminding him of the promise. Tran shrugged, a mere detail to be taken care of to rid himself of this prisoner. He leafed through numerous papers and extracted an oblong yellow sheet. Tran scanned the contents with exaggerated care. It seemed, he indicated, that his government had learned of the birth from International Red Cross sources.

Davidson screamed at the retreating figure. "You're lying, you're full-a-shit!" For the first time, that night he cried. He made no attempt to dam the flow of tears. He cried for his loss of innocence, for his loss of faith.

Another five days of torment before his next interview with Tran. He decided to bargain for more information. Tran had agreed to provide documentation at their next meeting. Davidson would be required to sign a confession and make a tape recording to secure such knowledge.

Strangely, only two agonizing days passed before he was escorted before Tran. Tran sat, as always, behind the table, small, fine hands clasped over a folded rectangle of yellow paper. Davidson ignored the blurred text of the confession placed before him on the table. He scribbled a signature, his mind a blank.

"Can I see the telegram now?" His throat dry, the words were scarcely audible. "First the recording, as we agreed." Hell, what's the use, he decided. I've already signed, the rationalization was easy. "Gimme the friggin' paper," he demanded, seething with hurt.

The interrogator withdrew the confession, substituting another text to be read onto tape. Davidson repeated the words in a dull monotone cadence. The thoughts, the words meant nothing. His eyes focused compulsively on the paper beneath the folded hands. It was over. It had been so simple.

Tran slid the paper across the table. Davidson's hands remained locked over his thigh muscles, refusing the final act of discovery. An indulgent smile on his face, Tran unfolded the paper. Davidson had to know. He knew that. But still, maybe not knowing was better. There could be hope. There could still be the fantasy he carried in his head.

He could not control himself. His emotions overpowered all reason. Tears flowed, blurring his vision. He blinked rapidly, shook his head, and looked down at the scrap of paper. It was all there, International Red Cross, daughter, Sarah.

Davidson knocked the chair back and stumbled from the hut, choking back gut-wrenching sobs. The walls of his cell pressed in, closer than he had ever felt before. His world became increasingly claustrophobic. Poised on the edge of insanity, he began to tap with ever-increasing ferocity, seeking, begging for human contact.

It took almost the entire night until Ramsey had all the details. That poor bastard, he thought, his mounting anger directed at Tran, the system, Nam. Furiously he began to send, telling Davidson it was all a lie, Tran's strategy. Over and over again, it's a lie, we know. We can help you.

Light began to filter into the cells. The guards were moving around, unlocking doors in preparation for the morning meal. The walls were silent, communication ended. As they were taken from their cells Ramsey sought a position near Davidson in the gathering line.

Davidson's eyes were rimmed with red and his face appeared more gaunt than ever before. However, he seemed more solid. His head was erect. He managed a small, laconic smile.

They moved through the wash ritual and started on the trail. Ramsey continued to whisper reassurances. Occasionally Davidson would raise his hand slightly or nod his head to acknowledge Ramsey's words. Throughout the morning's work the two leaders checked out Davidson, trying to gauge his attitude. By late morning Ramsey was convinced the man had made a decision to survive.

Davidson worked steadily, now and then lifting his head to gaze at the mountains and sky. At the noon break Ramsey was surprised to find Davidson first in line at the rear of the cart.

The work area was thirty yards from the trail. Davidson ate hungrily as he walked. All three guards had been extra-sensitive and attentive to their duties. Perhaps all the communication of the previous evening had made them edgy and suspicious.

Davidson indicated his empty bowl to Oahn and pointed to the cart. The guard nodded his assent. Davidson strolled casually toward the cart, passed the rear, and kept on going down the trail. Shit, thought

Ramsey, glancing at the guards. For the moment they were unaware of the retreating figure, eating their meal and conversing.

Davidson continued a slow, steady pace down the road. Oahn finally spotted him, his mouth dropped open. He remained frozen by the man's audacity and the ludicrous image of a prisoner ambling down a road in enemy territory.

Oahn rose, galvanized into action, and ran screaming after Davidson's receding image. He halted beside the cart and sighted his rifle. He screamed a final warning. There was no indication that Davidson heard or even cared.

The guard fired a single shot. The round impacted high on Davidson's right shoulder. He went down face forward in the dust. Ramsey said a silent prayer that he would stay still. Davidson pushed himself to one knee, blood pulsing down his back. He rose, the others could hear him groan with effort. Slowly he plodded forward.

Oahn moved the selector on his weapon and poured out an entire magazine at the stumbling figure. Davidson's body jerked violently, a bizarre dance of death in the dusty trail. Chunks of flesh exploded outward, ripped and torn by the streams of rounds.

The other two guards, visibly shaken, raised their weapons. They watched Davidson finally collapse like a deflated balloon. He lay crumpled, a small pathetic figure, leaking blood from a dozen wounds mingling with the dust of the trail.

Ramsey stood transfixed, absorbing the scene. Life went on despite the hollow, aching emptiness of his stomach. Insects still buzzed and swarmed around their heads. The sun rose still higher, burning down the valley, sapping their strength. They would probably spend the afternoon cutting brush.

Well fuck it, just fuck it, he raged inside. It's not how you die, it's how you live. We're all terminal, there is no dying, only life and death. Ramsey had chosen life, for the moment.

Oahn motioned for Ramsey and Wilson to follow him down the trail. They took the cart, the buffalo plodding along as his species had done for thousands of years. The body sprawled in the track, a quality of peace etched on the face. The two prisoners lifted Davidson and placed him gently in the cart. Mercifully, Oahn secured the work detail, probably to avoid any more trouble.

They humped slowly back to camp behind the cart. Ramsey would never forget the image of Davidson's head lolling back and forth, rocked by the swaying of the cart from side to side. The face was turned up to the sun, eyes open. Blood trickled from the open mouth, dripping and vanishing into dirt on the cart's floor.

The mood of the prisoners was subdued, sullen, and angry. Oahn stood in the rear of the cart, weapon leveled at the column of straggling men. The work party arrived at the compound. Tran and the commandant appeared immediately, demanding explanations for their unexpected appearance and break in the camp's routine.

Oahn indicated the body and launched into a lengthy, animated account. The commandant retired, already bored with the details. As the guard's story unfolded, Tran became more agitated.

Ramsey could read his mind. The asshole was worried because he had lost a prime collaborator. That was his big concern, the fury was building. Ramsey was pissed off, totally enraged. "You sneaky, sniveling, conniving little dog turd," he could not contain himself. The guards, already nervous and jumpy, were on him, beating and dragging his struggling body across the compound to the cages.

That night, as now, the bloody, dusty face of Davidson was clearly superimposed on his mind, clouding other thoughts and visions. There were others who had been lost, but Davidson was a tragic mistake. Ramsey held himself personally guilty. He should have recognized the man's naive vulnerability. Beneath the tough, brash veneer was someone untouched by reality and the cynicism of life. Everything was simple, the values clear; there was no gray, only black and white.

Through the mist and haze above the cage a few stars appeared, indistinct and blurred. Ramsey sighed and made a promise to the unforgiving world. If I ever get back, I'll look up Suzanne and try to explain. Try to tell her what a brave, innocent guy he was and how much he loved her.

Ramsey considered how he had relied on Cathy and her memory to fill the days of pain and nights of loneliness. It did not matter that there was no serious commitment or any future plans. She was part of his defense mechanism, an integral part.

Early in captivity he had divided his thoughts into three specific segments: emotional, logical, and sensual. Into these compartments he assigned his past life, the present, and the imagined future. His plan was to achieve a balance, exploring each area for a specific time each day.

In the early-morning hours on a work detail he might choose to be logical. He would construct a home or perhaps design a sailboat. The foundation or keel would be laid and timber by timber his structure would grow. Every detail would be painstakingly discussed and mulled over in his mind as he cut brush or planted rice.

In the afternoon he might send his mind as far back into childhood as he could remember. All the memories and events of his youth would live as visual pictures while he worked like a robot in the broiling sun and humidity.

Cathy he usually saved for the dark hours in his cell or the cage. Ramsey would even go as far as exploring her one sense at a time. Such thoughts of her smells, the feel of her body, provided many erotic moments.

At times, though, in the middle of his creations a sharp, wrenching pain settled in his guts. He tried to push the memory away, but still it persisted. It was at the end of his first tour....

13

THE LAND OF THE BIG PX

HE HAD rotated home. Dazed and uncomprehending, he rode the Freedom Bird. Within forty-eight hours, from humping in the boonies to stateside, the land of the Big PX. Grime from the field stuck under his nails and the smell of Nam clung to his flesh. There he was in summer khaki, medals, everything, ready to be a hero. They weren't ready for him, not even close.

He was uncomfortable, full of tension. Right from the start, at the airport in Los Angeles, he knew he was a stranger. People were wary of him, avoided making eye contact. The younger ones, his own age, regarded him with disgust, even open hostility.

In the lounge he caught vibes emanating from the next table. An attractive dark-haired girl was staring coldly at his decorations. Her male companion was trying to settle her down. She lifted her eyes to meet his own and spoke with utter contempt. "Hey, hero, you burn up any babies over there, maybe fuck over some old folks for fun?"

He was overwhelmed. Here was a girl, whom under other circumstances he might ask for a date, accusing him of atrocities. He rose, his whole body trembling. He tossed a couple of dollars on the table and stepped toward the couple. Looking straight into the brown eyes filled with hatred, he smiled and said, "Have a nice day."

Outside the bar he took deep breaths, trying to unknot his stomach. On the flight east the only friendly people he met were the stewardesses. There was an older guy who wanted to talk about his experiences in the "Big One."

The East Coast was not much better. He moved in a strange land, an alien out of synchronization with the environment. Unsure of himself, he hesitated to call Cathy from the airport. He decided it was foolishness on his part. They had something different, an understanding and respect for each other.

Her tone and words were neutral, devoid of emotion. She agreed to pick him up in an hour. Time to kill, he sat and observed the airport bustle. He was ignored almost totally except for a few inquisitive glances cast his way. A state trooper, former Marine, shook his hand and wished him well.

Ramsey spotted Cathy, her long legs flashing, weaving through the crowd. He had rehearsed this scene a hundred times, the joyous, passionate reunion. She stood before him now, searching his face. Forcing back his nervousness, he took her face in his hands and kissed her gently.

"Welcome home, at least you're safe." He wondered what that meant. He chose to ignore the qualified greeting and instead took her hand and guided them out of the building. The drive into the city was quiet, the atmosphere strained and subdued.

Ramsey was as nervous as an adolescent on a first date. He studied her profile as she drove. Sensing his eyes, she smiled, a small, sad ghost of an expression. She sighed and began, a low, shaky timbre to her voice.

"Jack, things change, people change. We can't pick up where we left off. You can't expect that." He waited for her to continue, sensing she had gone over these words before. "There are people and things going on in my life you wouldn't understand. You've changed, I've changed. I can't be the same."

Ramsey studied the winking lights of the city. Somehow he knew it would be like this. His disorientation was complete, an outsider lost in his own land. He wasn't angry, just immensely sad. It was as if he stood in the center of a small universe and the strings that held it all together were unraveling one by one.

"Cathy, I didn't ask for anything solid." He struggled for some clarity, the right words to make her understand. "All I need from you is a little love, not much at first. I need to know there is someone warm and caring, someone to trust. I guess what I'm asking is to be treated like a human being, not some blood-crazed monster."

Ramsey's plea shook with emotion. His voice rose, sounding harsh to his ears in the small car. "People have been looking at me as if I'm some kind of one-dimensional killer. Don't they know I have feelings, that I'm capable of love, that I can cry or laugh like anyone else?" He paused, drained and tired.

"Well, take off the damn uniform," she snapped across the widening distance. "I'm sorry, Jack, I shouldn't have said that. I'm confused. I don't know how I feel. It's too quick. One phone call and I'm supposed to change my life. I need time, Jack. I know it sounds like a cliché, but I need some time."

Ramsey rested his hand gently on her shoulder. "Look, Cathy, can't we, just for tonight, forget the uniform, the war, and be you and me, alone?"

He waited; the silence grew. "We can't, Jack, we can't. I wish we could. I've got a real hang-up about this war. Why did you have to go? You didn't have to, you know. It changed everything—my feelings, my ideas about you, about our relationship. I can't think of you as you were, knowing you took part in that shitty war."

Ramsey leaned back in the seat and closed his eyes. "Cathy, I don't want to fight or argue about the war or what I did over there. Can't we go someplace quiet and have dinner?" Again the prolonged quiet, broken only by traffic sounds.

"Jack, I can't go anywhere with you in uniform. You don't know, but it took a real effort to walk through that airport." Then, in a smaller, timid voice, "If you want to change we can stop by my place."

He was back in the boonies, humping a ridge line, the sun high. Faces of the dead paraded across his eyes. Friends and others, names remembered, names forgotten, a litany of faith stringing through his head. He was one of them, a boonie rat. Nothing on God's green planet could ever change that.

"Cathy, pull over please. I want to get out."

"Jack, let me take you home."

"Why, Cat? So you won't feel so guilty?"

She looked at him quickly, eyes full. "I'm not sure I should feel guilty."

"Fine, so pull over, please."

She eased the car out of traffic and stopped. She leaned across and kissed his rigid cheek. "Ramsey, please give me some time, a couple of weeks, okay? Call me, please. I'm sorry it had to be like this, honest. So please call. I think I..." Her words were lost. He was out the door, dragging his seabag from the rear.

Shouldering his bag, he walked rapidly down the street, afraid of what he might do or say. Fifty yards away he turned. She stood facing him, a hand covering her mouth.

He held his breath, then exhaled slowly. A boonie rat phrase came almost automatically. It don't mean nothin', it don't mean nothin', just drive on. Ramsey turned and continued on down the sidewalk, heading for the heart of the city. The seabag grew heavier. Finally he stopped and hailed the first cab he saw.

On the ride home he pretended to be asleep, avoiding any potential conversation. The folks were predictably happy to see him, fussing, piling food on his plate. They asked about everything, health, future plans, everything but the war. The subject was taboo. They were afraid of what they might hear. Push it into the background, pretend it doesn't exist.

He excused himself, claiming jet lag, and climbed the stairs to his old room. He was in fact emotionally and mentally exhausted. Sleep came easily—no agonizing images, no dreams, just blessed nothingness.

The rising sun streamed in his window. He was instantly awake. Confused by his surroundings, he lay still in his uniform, minus shoes. Then it hit him, the realization he had nothing to do, no place to go. Well, that's what I'll do, he thought—nothing, for at least a week.

The whole idea of having no controls, no obligations, was exhilarating, yet tinged with fear. He lay staring at the ceiling, thinking of his previous evening. Cathy's face floated before his eyes. He could accept how she felt. She was naive, everything could be labeled right or wrong. On the other hand he couldn't understand the rejection of everything they had experienced together. You couldn't wipe all that out and pretend it never happened.

Ah well, movin' on from here, he sighed, rising from the bed. He looked at the pillow and the sheets, ran hot water over his hands in the bathroom, and shook his head. Funny, things we take as given. He looked at the strange, gaunt face in the mirror.

Breakfast was a repeat performance of the night before. Food a substitute for emotion, pile it on; the more you eat, the better and healthier your outlook on life. His folks chattered away, filling any silence. He began to wonder if it was his imagination, but he sensed the whole scene was artificial.

He began to doubt his own perception of reality. He felt his parents moving warily around him, afraid to penetrate or disturb his particular mood. They were checking out his reaction to every particle of conversation. Ramsey felt like an invalid or a newly released mental patient. He had to get away.

Once outside the house, on the pretense of checking out the old neighborhood, he couldn't make up his mind whether to go right or left. He walked aimlessly in the quiet morning. A screen door slammed, his body tensed, ready to go into a crouch. He laughed, embarrassed and sweating. On down the street, stopping at the familiar grocery store.

Ramsey had known old man Cicerone since fifth grade. The aging Italian shook his hand and called him Jackie. Again Ramsey tried to analyze his own thoughts. Was it really pity he saw in the old man's eyes or just tearful acceptance of his homecoming?

So it went for the days that followed. Neighbors, friends, he kept trying to get beneath the surface. What were they really thinking and feeling? He felt they were treating him as they would a family heirloom. Careful, careful, it's delicate, be sure to avoid any rough handling.

Or the other extreme. The bolder ones, "You kill any gooks over there?" That was it, a simple question requiring a simple response. Nothing deeper than the surface. They didn't want to hear about the reality of the war. They tuned him out when he tried to talk about the disturbing effects the conflict was causing for a lot of guys.

On his third night home he went into the city. He rented a room in a rundown hotel. About ten o'clock and half a bottle of Scotch later he left his room and began a round of the strip joints up and down the street. The whole evening was a blurry mess. He tried to piece the night together in the morning. She was blonde and tall, like Cathy. Arguments, fights, he felt soiled, used, sick and depressed.

It was time for some positive action in his life.

The campus seemed much the same. The kids had longer hair and their clothes were bizarre, but that was okay, no big deal. He could live with that, no problem.

The dean, a dignified white-haired gentleman, assured him there would be no trouble in resuming his studies the coming semester. Then the man got nervous and evasive. He rambled on about veterans' groups, adjustment seminars, free speech movements. Ramsey tried to clarify the digression. The dean was hinting, in a roundabout manner, that he might experience some difficulty readjusting to life at the university.

After the interview he roamed around the campus visiting his old hangouts. Physically, nothing had changed. The attitude was different. The kids were loose, free, less purposeful than he remembered.

This was not an ivy-league type university. You came here for an immediate, employable skill. As he observed these students, he was struck by their obvious lack of concern over the university's schedule. They gathered in groups rapping, others sat around musicians playing flutes or guitars. He detected a strong odor of grass hanging in the air. Well, that's fine with me, he thought, each to his own. Jesus, I'm one magnanimous liberal since I got back; he laughed softly to the quadrangle of buildings.

He stopped in the Student Union cafeteria for coffee. The huge room was packed. He leaned against the wall, wondering if anyone went to class. Anti-war posters decorated the walls.

In one corner a young woman standing on a chair was delivering an impassioned speech. Over the noise Ramsey caught fragmented parts of the oration: Dow Chemical, inhumane, napalm. A young bearded man offered Ramsey a leaflet and moved on through the crowd.

The plans for a sit-in demonstration were outlined on the paper. When the armed forces recruiting officers visited the campus their booths were to be surrounded by a mass of bodies.

"Pretty good tactic, huh?" a thin, bespectacled girl in a granny dress to his right offered in comment, then added, "It'll keep any poor suckers who are thinking about signing up away from the warmongers."

Ramsey couldn't help himself. "Personally, I think if you want to be a poor sucker and sign up, you've got every right." The girl looked at him as if he had uttered a gross obscenity. She shook her head in disgust and moved away. He pushed his way through the crowd into the sunlight.

Ramsey took to his room for longer periods of time. He would sit in a chair by the window trying to place himself someplace solid and understandable. The school situation was tentative. He wasn't sure he could remain aloof and untouched by all the turmoil. How to cope with Cathy, should he call? Another unanswered question, and the folks watching for signs of disturbance or whatever they thought might take place.

Tired of his room, he walked the streets for hours at a time. He began truly to withdraw, avoiding any kind of contact beyond the minimal superficial level. It wasn't real life, it was merely functioning.

More and more he visualized himself back in the boonies. Logically, he knew it made no sense to relive the experience, all the operations, all the firefights. But in these retreats to the past he felt emotionally alive. At least you knew who you were and what to expect. Ramsey slowly came to the truth he almost dreaded to discover. He missed the rush of contact, the anticipation of a tree line erupting with fire. He missed the whole aura and atmosphere of Nam. He hated and feared the place, but also there was a need to be there. A love of walking the thin line between life and death.

So it came to pass, on a Monday afternoon following a long weekend of calculated self-indulgence, that he re-enlisted. The old gunnery sergeant fixed him with a knowing smile. "Those civilian shitheads don't know nothin', Ramsey. They don't know what it's all about. They run around worryin' their sorry asses off, thinkin' life is tough."

The gunny had been at Chosin in Korea. He was strictly old Corps. He settled back in his chair, cigar clamped in the corner of his mouth, his hands clasped behind his head, ready to deliver thoughts he had been saving for the right occasion.

"You're a friggin' dinosaur, Ramsey. Your kind has gone outta style. They don't want you around. If you lived in Japan you'd be a fuckin' samurai, a warrior. Here, they want us to do their fightin' for 'em, but they don't want to see us or hear about what's happenin' out there in the boonies."

The air was thick with smoke as the old grunt puffed angrily on his cigar. "Believe me, Ramsey, this is the worst friggin' thing that has ever happened to the Marine Corps. Ya know why? Because the public believes all that shit they see and hear on television is real. After this is over they're gonna run our asses through the meat grinder. There's gonna be a hundred million Monday-mornin' quarterbacks out there."

The gunny paused for breath, waving his cigar for emphasis. Abruptly he stopped. He had spent himself and felt a little embarrassed by the vehemence of his tirade. "Well, shit, enough of that, won't solve anythin'. Let's get you processed."

Once the decision was made, he felt some kind of peace. He tried to explain to his folks. They didn't understand. He called Cathy. She was hysterical, screaming and crying on the telephone. Ramsey took the phone from his ear and reluctantly placed it back on the cradle.

On the flight to Okinawa the majority of the passengers were new guys, replacements. There were four troopies, including himself, who had been in country before. He recognized them immediately. They had the cool, resigned look, the thousand-yard stare. They didn't laugh nervously or talk too loudly.

At Da Nang he caught a chopper to Division Headquarters. From there he would be lifted in to Recon's area of operation. That simple, from potential civilian to a green machine in less than a week....

14

THE RAINS

HUDDLED AGAINST the cold in a corner of the cage, he knew the decision had been inevitable. Sure, he wouldn't be freezing his ass off and fighting rats, but that was all the luck of the draw. He was not the type to dwell on might-have-beens. Once a move was made, you did your best.

That was the attitude with which he approached the decision to escape. He was going, no doubt in his mind. He would give it his best shot or die in the attempt.

Time for sleep, the sky was shading black to gray. The days passed slowly. Ramsey anxiously scanned the mountaintops for telltale signs of the coming rains.

He tried to plan the infraction that would merit cage time within the first few days of the monsoon. Tran was beginning to tire, his patience growing thin with Ramsey's evasiveness. The interrogator had begun to display uncharacteristic emotional outbursts, unaware that Ramsey was strung out, nearing the edge, close to mental collapse. It would have to be a minor insult, nothing major. Tran might lose his cool, get totally out of control, and ship him north.

The interrogator's tactics had modified slowly in the past few months. Formerly, he had hung on to prisoners as long as possible, seeking and probing for a weakness. Maybe, just maybe, old Tran was getting tired of the war. The last few sessions with him had been threatening.

In the old days he would lecture patiently, refuting any counterargument effectively. He almost convinced Ramsey, in one particular bout, that the involvement in Vietnam was due to the American preoccupation with racial and intellectual supremacy.

"Your people consider that because an individual is yellow, black, or some shade in between, he or she must automatically be primitive or intellectually inferior." Ramsey began to protest but lapsed into silence, realizing Tran was really going to run with this one.

"When you burn a village, don't you know the people experience emotions of hate, fear, and sadness? Do you think they feel nothing, Ramsey? Answer me," he demanded. Ramsey conceded his argument had some measure of validity.

Since then Tran had begun to insult and goad him into angry responses. Ramsey had the feeling his time was short. Tran was either going to force him to capitulate in some way or send him north. It was a question of being able to judge the man's patience.

Perhaps if he gave a little. If he kept Tran happy for the next few weeks, he would have a chance. He had to protect himself and the plan. Another five days gone and still no rains. He was so eager for their passing that they seemed to double in length. The only relief was communicating with Swanson and the others.

Swanson had agreed to create some kind of diversion. The others had likewise offered to cooperate. Ramsey had become a symbol. If they could help him it would be proof of their own desire to resist. They began to slip him portions of their meals whenever the guards were occupied.

Ramsey was divided. On one hand he was overwhelmed by their sacrifice. Food was enormously important to survival. At the same time, he did not wish to share any details of his scheme. The more people who knew of his plan, the better the chance of betrayal.

Ramsey began to watch Kidd, whom he suspected of collaborating. Kidd had been captured outside Hue during the battle for the city. From the beginning he had been reluctant to communicate, especially after a night in the cage.

They knew very little about Kidd beyond his physical appearance. He was average in almost every aspect, he would go unnoticed in a room or on the street. Kidd avoided looking at any of the other prisoners. His pale watery eyes fixed on the ground or off in the distance.

Ramsey tried to get near him on the work details. Kidd managed to slip away, closer to the guards. Ramsey had only wanted to talk, to reason with Kidd, even ask his cooperation. He thought this might be a chance to pull him back into the fold.

Finally, frustrated by Kidd's questionable behavior, he took a chance and tapped out an open and concise message on his cell wall. "Kidd, one word and you're dead meat. Ramsey." He knew the message would be passed along the network. He really did not expect an answer. There was none; the walls remained silent and foreboding.

All the next day he eyeballed Kidd, looking for some reaction. Nothing, absolutely nothing, the man was in a world of his own. When the work detail returned to camp, Tran asked for Ramsey before the evening meal. The timing was irregular.

He walked behind the guard, rage and fear mingling in the pit of his stomach. Kidd talked, the bastard squealed, the thought ran through his head. Got to be careful, he cautioned himself, keep your shit together, buddy. Deny everything, turn it around, Kidd is lying to gain favor. He picked me because I'm a malcontent. He formulated his replies and entered the hut.

"Sergeant Ramsey," Tran had dropped the veneer of the polite instructor. "Your stay with us has been most unproductive. You, Wilson, and Swanson have done nothing of a positive nature. In fact, you have hindered my efforts to help the other prisoners."

Tran was visibly agitated, his normally placid face taut and hard. His fingers drummed a tattoo on the table. "I can do nothing more. My superiors are demanding results."

Ramsey felt his heart lift with excitement. He doesn't know. Kidd hadn't talked. The escape was safe. Oh baby, just get me through this session and I'm long gone. That was, if the rains arrived on schedule. He struggled to keep his face devoid of the joyous emotion bubbling inside.

The interrogator's tone became increasingly sarcastic. "You know how it is as a lowly sergeant, everything flows downhill." Tran leaped to his feet, leaned across the table, and spat the words into Ramsey's face. "You, Ramsey, you are the one who will be covered in shit, not me. Do you understand? I refuse, I absolutely refuse to be responsible for your stupidity."

Tran sat, grasping the arms of the chair in a semblance of control. This dude is under some kind of pressure. Ramsey eyed him warily, calculating a response. "I'll explain, Sergeant, so that even you might understand. The next convoy to the north is in three weeks. From now on we will have daily sessions. Should you fail to make progress, you will be handed over to Oahn after we meet. Then you will spend every night in solitary confinement."

Tran was building to a climax, driven on by his fury. "If, by the time the convoy arrives, you and I have failed to agree, you will leave, marked as incorrigible. That means, officially, you will cease to exist. You will become a laborer in the tin mines and work there till you die."

The tirade ended, Tran folded his arms tightly across his chest. Ramsey's mind spun like a roulette wheel, seeking the correct answer that would pay off with a reprieve. All his cunning and battle sense clicked into operation. On a giant screen at the back of his head the word "survive, survive" kept flashing in brilliant colors.

When he finally spoke, the words appeared to be rational and sincere. "Tran, I understand your predicament. I am sure you can, as an educated man, understand my position. Death is something I do not seek."

Ramsey continued hesitantly, choosing his words carefully. "My resistance is based not on the Code of

Conduct, but on a belief in myself." The interrogator appeared to be listening, eyes half-closed, staring at a point somewhere above Ramsey's head. "For me to collaborate would mean surrendering a part of my being," Ramsey continued, displaying what he hoped would be perceived as genuine emotion.

"But again, I do not wish to die. Allow me one week to decide how much of myself I can surrender in order to live. One week and you will have my final decision."

The air was still and heavy, disturbed only by insect sounds and the breathing of the two men. Sweat rolled freely down Ramsey's back and sides. Through the window behind Tran, Ramsey could see great black rolling clouds move over the mountain peaks. Ramsey's body shivered, a finger of lightning crackled down the valley. Rain splattered on the roof, slowly at first, then, gaining momentum, arrived in a solid sheet obscuring the view from the window.

Come on, asshole, come on, prayed Ramsey, give me the right answer. Tran stood. Turning his back, he watched the downpour. He spoke to the rain. "Three days, Ramsey, no more. Go!" Ramsey had difficulty containing his elation. He adopted a slumped, humble posture and shuffled toward the door.

Outside, he turned his face up to the rain and closed his eyes. The glorious liquid filled his mouth. Ramsey laughed and gagged as he stumbled across the muddy compound. The bedraggled guard regarded this crazy man with suspicion, urging him forward.

Ramsey would not be denied. He executed clumsy pirouettes over the slick ground, slipping and sliding. He lost his footing and collapsed laughing in the mud. The impatient guard unslung his rifle. Ramsey scrambled to his feet, raising his hands, palms outward. "Take it easy. I'm goin', I'm goin'." Still smiling and laughing quietly, he made his way through the torrent to the cellblock....

15
LEAVE-TAKING

THE EUPHORIA faded in the dark confining atmosphere of his cell. Ramsey lay on his rank-smelling blanket and thought through the session. He had bought some time with his promise, but what else? If he failed to deliver, Oahn would have his long-awaited chance to destroy him. He would be in no condition to make the attempt. He must get himself into the cage within the next few days.

The best bet would be a simple insult to Tran or one of the guards, except, of course, Oahn. He would take the chance that any physical punishment would not be too severe. He made the decision. If the rains continued, he must go the following evening.

The other problem was Swanson and Wilson. They were in the same boat as Ramsey. Tran would present them with the same dilemma—cooperate or accept slow death. He decided to lay low for the evening, not willing to risk the transmission of such important information to the others.

He did, however, send "Swanson, need to talk tomorrow, Ramsey." He began for the thousandth time to review his plan. But he had fallen asleep before he managed to escape the cage. The steady rhythm of the rain fixed a smile on his lips.

By the water pump after morning chow Swanson caught Ramsey's attention and nodded slightly. The torrential rain of the night had given way to a steady misting drizzle. The line of men fell in on the road. Ramsey took a place directly behind Swanson. They moved out, slipping through the mud on the trail.

Ramsey said a silent prayer of thanks. All three guards had squeezed into the cart. They had obviously decided not to wallow through the mud with the prisoners.

Ramsey immediately began to whisper softly. "Swanson, bad news. Tran's gonna send you and Wilson north to the tin mines unless you give within the next three weeks. He's gonna let Oahn beat the shit out of you until convoy time. When Oahn's through, cage duty every night. Catch my drift?"

Swanson shook his head from side to side. "Oh man, how did I ever get myself into this lashup? You get the same deal?"

Ramsey felt a deep affinity for the proud black man. He hesitated with his plan. "Yeah, I got the same shit. Swanson, I'm goin' tonight. I don't want you to help. You got enough problems, okay? I can make it on my own."

A hundred yards of silence. "Don't mean nothin' to me. Fuck it, drive on man, do your stuff. But don't tell me how I gotta act. I'll do what I feel like, Ramsey. Got it?"

Ramsey plodded on down the trail. He wanted to reach out and touch the man in front, wanted to make physical contact to let him know the extent of his emotion. Ramsey knew if he did that Swanson would get totally pissed off. He would not allow his tough street shell to be penetrated.

He felt a comradeship with Swanson that was stronger than he had ever experienced with another human being. All during the day his emotions bubbled at the surface. He found himself on the verge of weeping as he worked. They had been through so much together. No one could ever understand the bond that had been forged through suffering and enduring.

Ramsey tried to compose the appropriate words to say good-by. Nothing came to mind. Swanson would die. He would never break in the time allotted by

Tran. He would slowly wither away, a mole deep under a tin mountain.

He started to panic as the small procession neared camp at the close of the workday. The rain was heavier now, dense mist swirled and settled in the valley. The miserable line of prisoners gathered around the water pump. Then it hit him. He chuckled softly at the bizarre idea that popped into his mind.

Swanson had finished washing as much mud as he could from his body. He turned to go. Ramsey stepped in front, dropped to his knees, arms raised, hands reaching up to the leaden sky. "Swanee, Swanee, how I love ya, how I love ya, my dear old Swanee."

Prisoners and guards alike froze, stunned by the ridiculous image of Ramsey shaking his hands and singing at the top of his lungs. Over and over he belted out the chorus. Swanson, hands on hips, was shaking his head and laughing. "You're a goddamn maniac, Ramsey. You've finally flipped, right round the friggin' bend."

Tran appeared on the porch, screaming at the guards. They grabbed the outstretched arms and dragged him, still singing, backward through the mud to the cage. Swanson, framed by the bars, was entering the cellblock. He turned to look at Ramsey and jerked his thumb up into the air....

16
ESCAPE

So it began. He sat in the unrelenting torrent filled with nervous tension. The rain and clouds sweeping down off the mountains created a premature dusk. The camp was still, drawing in, seeking shelter from the thrumming downpour. Normally the October monsoons depressed and agitated Ramsey. Not now. The anticipation was pumping him up to a heightened state of eagerness.

He braced himself against the uphill wall of the cage. With his heel he began to scour a channel along its soft floor. The loose, wet earth gave way easily. Within a short period of time he had dug a channel three or four inches deep.

Then he started from the corners, again on the upslope, and dug with his hands toward the channel. When he had finished, he was sitting between the arms of a Y leading down the slope of the hill. Runoff from the hill followed the pattern and soon filled and widened the trenches.

He rose and stepped carefully to the lower end of the cage. Again with his feet he gouged a depression in the earth across the face of the hill. This newest excavation was the length covered by three bamboo bars.

Ramsey then connected the main channel with the depression. He watched satisfied as the rainwater washed around the base of the upright poles. He estimated the bars to be sunk two feet into the soil. Once it was fully dark he would unearth his digging stick and begin in earnest.

Now the waiting began. Ramsey relaxed, surveying his handiwork, occasionally moving earth here or there with his feet. To his delight, the rains continued with ever-increasing intensity. After dark he would need to make one drainage channel outside the cage. The water around the bars had to be kept circulating.

As it was now, the water was filling the depression and leaking over the downhill edges. He had to keep it moving and exiting from one spot to ensure good erosion of the earth.

Through the curtain of rain two hunched figures sloshed toward the cage. Evening meal; the guard was angry with his assignment. Soaked and miserable, he urged the prisoner carrying it down the hill. Ramsey had been sure the guard would not take time to check the cage.

He was right. The bowl was thrust into his hands. A whispered message was snatched away by the rain and the guard dragging the prisoner back. The door slammed quickly and the dim figures retreated through the murk to the compound.

Ramsey quickly ate the soggy rice and vegetables before the bowl was completely filled with rainwater. Licking his fingers, he smiled, a secret, satisfied expression on his rain-soaked face. He hefted the empty bowl, calculating its contribution to his plan. Ramsey had already foreseen the bowl as another intricate cog in his scheme. The guard would not, as was customary, return to retrieve it.

The monsoon reduced the guards' activity to only the minimal necessities needed to maintain vigilance. A simple bowl would not be high on the list of dangerous implements. With the bowl and digging stick, Ramsey felt sure he could dig out from under the bars.

On a night such as this there would be no moon or stars. The heavy, swirling clouds seemed to reach almost to ground level. The water continued to cascade down the slope, washing around his rear end and feet splayed in the mud.

One corner of his mind knew it was futile, but still another part held out a sly, furtive hope. He dug up the food cache from the left hand high corner of the cage. The cloth bundle was rotted through. A few grains of rice and fat white maggots dropped in his lap, the cloth disintegrating with his touch. Shit, what did you expect? he asked. Not one of the better ideas I ever had. Still, his spirits were not deflated.

The continued torrent rushing through the cage buoyed his hopes and gave credence to his plan. The light was gone now, the lower end of the cage barely visible. Turning his head, Ramsey could not distinguish the camp buildings. The guard on the porch, if there was one, would not be able to observe his activity.

What the hell is that? His head snapped around. Incredible. The sound of voices raised in song coming from the cellblock. Swanson, he knew it immediately. An attempt to keep the guards occupied inside. The words were hardly distinguishable, but Ramsey caught snatches of the hymns of each military service, then regular hymns. The singing would cease, then begin again.

Time to move, get the digging stick. He reached between the bars, dislodging earth from the incline beyond the hole he had dug. Water began draining. He drove the stick deeper and deeper. Got myself a regular Mississippi delta system, he laughed, increasing his efforts.

He reached into the hole, feeling down the length of the bamboo poles. They were still solidly embedded in the soil, but he had made progress. He judged the time to be about ten o'clock. His plan was to be out by two and into the river by three. A good two hours or so of floating downstream in darkness, then crawl into the jungle, resting and hiding during the daylight hours.

Flashes of lightning briefly lit up the valley. He lost all sense of caution and began frantically scooping water and mud with the food bowl. After fifteen minutes he flopped backward, face upturned to the rain. With his toes he felt down into the hole. His big toe passed under the bottom of two bars. The third was still sunk in the hill.

Rousing himself, he resumed the attack. Talking quietly all the while, he worked to a silent cadence. "This is it, mother, all you've waited for. Dig. Dig, shithead, dig. Vietnam sucks. Dig, dig." On he went, inside and outside the bars, scraping, pushing the earth and water down the slope.

Please don't stop, rain, please, he silently prayed. Mud and rain obscured his vision. He had to pause and free his eyes of muck and grime. Reaching down and under the bars, he attacked the loose earth outside.

He decided to experiment. Lowering his legs into the hole, he slid forward. He was able to move legs and groin under the bars. He sucked in his breath and pushed. Shit! A silent scream. He panicked, impaled, the bars holding him painfully in place.

The water swirled around his face. He pulled his belly up, back against his backbone, and slid free, returning to the cage. Breathing deeply, his heart fluttering, he closed his eyes against the rain.

He might have slept. He did not know. A strange sensation, an awareness of his surroundings came to his consciousness. It was quiet, no drumming of rain. Tentative insect sounds buzzed and clicked from the jungle. Light pockets appeared in the heavy overcast.

Ramsey was instantly alert. The rain had gone. Compound buildings drifted back and forth in the mist clinging to the ground. He debated the choice. Go on or quit? He had nothing to lose. What the fuck else can they do to me? he rationalized.

Resolved and ignoring the camp behind, he began digging steadily. He did not stop for rest but continued on and on, ignoring the pain of his cramped body. Through the broken clouds light from a half-moon illuminated the surrealistic scene. A ragged, mud-covered apparition clawing its way to a surface of light.

Again he felt under the poles. He could do it now, he was sure. Ramsey gripped the bars with both hands, took a deep breath, and slid downward. He felt the rough edges scrape up along his stomach. The water rose steadily as he sank into the hole.

Fighting the urge to go totally berserk, he allowed his head to sink beneath the surface. His chin caught beneath one of the uprights. Forcing his skull back into the slime, he relieved the pressure on his jaw. He dug his heels into the slope, bent his knees, and pulled forward. At the same time his hands pulled and clawed at the loose earth, seeking purchase.

Water and mud ran into his inverted nostrils. He couldn't last much longer. Fighting down his terror, he lifted his head. Nothing, he was under. He flipped over on his stomach and backed down, out of the hole. He slid further down the slick incline.

He was out! Sweet Jesus, he was out, alone and free! For one peaceful, eternal moment he lay, arms reaching to the sky. He wanted to scream out in triumph. Instead, he exhaled a great blast of silent exhilaration and pounded his fists into the saturated earth.

Once rid of this emotion, bush sense took over. Like a giant slug he slithered down the slope into the jungle. Never, never had the green looked so glorious. He had humped and hated through this stuff for months at a time, loathing every step.

Now, sliding under the protective canopy, he grasped and coveted every friendly root and vine. Down, down he went to the valley floor, scuttling and clawing like a crab. It had been this way in the dreams. Could it be true? Could he make it happen? Even as he collided with trees and stumbled over roots, he laughed hysterically. Oh my fuckin' word, I'm free, I'm free!

He stopped to rest. He guessed he was halfway

to the river. He sat, head on his knees. A large bubble of something settled in his chest. He found himself sobbing, gasping mouthfuls of air as the emotional balloon beneath his ribs slowly deflated.

On down through the foothills, mosquitoes swarming. A silvery ribbon, caught by the moon, vaguely glimpsed, perhaps half an hour away. He hoped it would rain again, covering his tracks. It really didn't matter. He was committed. If he was captured it was all over, the end of his existence.

In spite of the cool dankness of the air, he was sweating heavily. The descent became more difficult, the jungle dense and harder to penetrate. Shafts of moonlight stabbed through the thick cover overhead at irregular intervals. Ramsey sought these islands of light, moving from one to the other in the general direction of the valley floor. A sharp cracking sound froze him in midstride. Holding his breath, he sank to one knee. He was absolutely still. Then more crashing sounds, retreating through the jungle to his right. He exhaled slowly, relaxing. A large animal must have been startled by his approach.

He stumbled on, fighting his way through the clinging brush. The ground was gradually beginning to level. He must be getting close. Thorns tore at his already tattered clothing. His feet were bloody, the primitive sandals forgotten, left behind in the cage.

At times he moved in total darkness, oblivious to the brush slashing at his face and outstretched arms.

His headlong rush to the river halted when his foot encountered nothing but air. He pitched forward down an embankment. Fortunately, the bottom of the small ravine was spongy, covered with thick wet moss.

Ramsey's pride suffered more than his body. "Asshole, stupid shit, slow down. You're gonna do Charlie's job for him. Get your act together," he hissed into the black void of night. Forcing himself to loosen up, he sat thinking.

He estimated he had been free about an hour. The reality of the thought careened and banged around inside his head. Even in the darkness, with the jungle pressing in on every side, he experienced an invigorating sense of freedom. Me, me, he thought, no one else in control. That's what it meant to be free.

It was his decision. He could at any point in the coming days give up and wait for death. But that alternative was insane. He knew he would push to the very end. The other certainty was that he would not allow himself to be captured again.

17

THE RIVER

CALM AND assured, he pushed on slowly and carefully toward the river. Again, sounds seeping through the night. Ramsey, immobile, listened, straining to identify them. Low, soft, constant murmuring like muted conversation. Then it came, a joyous recognition.

It was the river, the good old goddamn, sluggish, dirty brown river, twenty yards away. Ramsey glimpsed the dull surface reflecting moonlight. He negotiated the final slope. There it was. The first part of the journey was over. It didn't look quite as impressive as he had imagined. But now the dream was reality.

Viewed from inside the cage, sunlight had danced across its surface. The pale ribbon had looped in sensuous curves. Now he saw the cruddy reddish-brown water, trimmed along the bank by dingy foam. Debris was scattered everywhere across the surface, washed down from higher elevations.

Large pieces of brush, leaves, and tree limbs slowly floated past. Would he be carried to the sea or, like much of the flotsam, be hung up on the bank to rot in the rain and sun?

Ramsey pushed the thought away and waded into the river. He was surprised by its warmth in contrast to the chill of the air. The current tugged around his knees. When the water reached his waist and he had firm footing, he turned, facing upstream.

In his plan he had envisioned a sturdy log to support his weight. This would allow him to float placidly downstream. Thin pieces of brush swirled by, but nothing substantial appeared.

On to Plan B, he mused. Can't stand in the middle of this river all night. So resolved, he sank down to his neck and lifted his feet. Floating on his back, he stared up at the rapidly moving clouds punctuated by gaps of clear sky. Now and then stars winked through the overcast, friendly pinpoints of solace to the upturned face.

He was tired. It took all his powers of concentration to maintain position. The current was stronger in the middle of the river, and there was the added danger of floating junk moving swiftly around his body. Twice in the first ten minutes he had to fight free of clinging, scratching vegetation.

Still, it would keep him awake. Even if he went under, he would immediately awaken. Thoughts and images flickered behind his eyes. So peaceful, ears submerged, a state of nonbeing. He wondered if death was like this tranquillity.

What if God Himself were looking down at this small white spot shimmering in a sea of darkness? What would the Creator think or do, or even care? Give him peace and protect him on the way to the sea? Or, as Ramsey had chosen to believe all his life, leave him to his own devices.

Then he began to worry about the types of animals and reptiles that inhabited the river. Snakes and leeches, he knew for sure, having encountered them before. But what else? Suppose all around were sharp-fanged or poisonous creatures lurking, waiting for a chance at his flesh?

It was the same eerie feeling he got diving off a boat into deep water. What was down there, prowling below the surface? This is stupid, he thought. What the hell does it matter? I have no choice but to go on and take what's offered.

He was getting cold, beginning to lose sensation in his hands and feet. It was at least another hour or more to first light. They would begin to hunt shortly after dawn. Had he left tracks or signs for them to follow? Probably, he guessed, but to search the jungle on both banks of the river all the way to the sea would be physically impossible. By the time the search began he would be safely hidden, resting and preparing for the next night.

The cold was seeping inward from his extremities. Gotta start my engines here, he told himself, turning over onto his stomach. Ramsey began a rhythmic breast stroke. After swimming for a while he felt the blood start moving again. He was revitalized, tingling, cutting through the water at good speed.

He tried to calculate the distance he had traveled. From his sailing days he gauged the current at approximately two knots. His time in the river so far was about an hour and a half. Add to that fact, he was swimming now, gaining maybe half a knot. He had to be at least two miles downstream. If he could stay in the water another hour or so he could clock up five miles.

His thoughts were dispelled by a stunning blow at the base of his skull. He went under, dazed and confused. Rising to the surface, choking and spitting, he tried to reorient himself.

He was tangled in a large tree limb. The trunk itself was as thick as his thigh. Three or four branches remained attached. Here's my raft, he thought, gratefully wrapping his arms around the trunk.

He struggled to position his body over the length of the tree. The limb sank and his progress slowed.

Well, let's see now, he considered the problem. Inching his body backward, he raised the downstream end of the branch. Once the bow of his raft broke the surface, forward movement resumed at a more efficient pace.

Not great, he thought, but at least we're movin' and I can save some energy. He hung on, not resting his whole weight on the limb. On down the river he floated, exhausted but secure for the moment, satisfied that he was moving farther and farther away from the camp.

He was cold and miserable, but knew the work detail would be leaving without him this morning. That in itself was enough to keep him going. He tried to stay alert, watching the river bank for any sign of human habitation. There was none. The jungle pressed in on the river, each side a wall of green darkness.

As the elevation dropped, the current would slow and the jungle recede. This would probably mean he would pass villages as the river approached the sea. The river delta system would feed into rice paddies and near the mouth would be fishing villages.

Where there were fishermen, there were boats. That was his only hope—some type of craft he could sail, paddle, or even one that would just float him out to sea.

Ahead, the river narrowed, passing through a gorge. The sides were steep, some ancient rock formation the river had failed to erode. Now he could hear the rapids and see white water, the rock walls squeezing in on the river.

Ramsey had to make a decision instantly. He could either try for the bank before the rapids and find his way around, or ride the fragile raft and hope for the best. Unwilling to give up his hospitable limb, he tightened his grip and said a quick prayer.

The speed of the branch doubled, pulled forward into the boiling turbulence. In the pale light he could see the waves rebounding off the rock walls into those following behind. Mist hung over the surging river.

Ramsey slid back, his head well behind the bow of the craft. He closed his eyes and hung on like death. The water slapped and tore at his body. The raft sought a path through the maelstrom. His body jarred, the limb had struck a rock. He was swept sideways, buffeted by the storm, and scraped along the side of a boulder.

The limb was gone. The current rolled and tumbled him like an abandoned surfboard. His fingers sought a hold of some type—anything, a rock, the bottom. He plunged on, now submerged, now tossed into the air gasping, fighting for breath.

He knew he must protect his head. He lost count of the blows to other portions of his body. Knees scraped over submerged rocks. Elbows and hips collided with boulders. The rushing water twisted and pulled, searching for the fastest passage through the ravine.

He went under again, deeper, the water colder. Struggling to gain the surface, he became disoriented and confused by the tumbling motion of his body. His lungs were empty. Frantically he strove to fight back the panic paralyzing his brain. Black spots whirled behind his eyes. His rear end bounced along the bottom. Gathering his feet and legs beneath, he uncoiled and shot toward the surface.

His head broke free. The river was spreading and slowing. He was through. Turning on his back, he filled his lungs with sweet, pure air. Okay, I give, he thought, time to call it a night. He peered ahead, down the course of the river. A small point jutted out from the left-hand bank before the river swept around the next loop. Expending his last reserve of strength, he fought his way out of the current's force.

His destination was a jumble of gnarled, interlaced roots reaching down into the dark water. The river had eroded the ground beneath the banks of the point, leaving many of the trees hanging precariously. Tangled vines dipped their fingers down into the water.

Ramsey threaded his way through the snarled mass of vegetation and gradually pulled himself above the water level. The undergrowth was so thick, he had to crawl on his belly to the center of the point. There the ground was solid and the foliage not so dense.

He lay semiconscious like a shipwrecked sailor thrown up on a beach. He longed for blessed sleep and warmth. His shivering, aching body would not permit him to rest. He rose to his feet, determined to find some place of comfort.

The sky was beginning to assume paler shades, forecasting the coming dawn. He could not distinguish the detail of his surroundings. He crept forward through the tangled growth. Beyond the river bank the terrain rose gradually.

He came upon a rock face rising out of the jungle. Feeling his way to the right, he encountered nothing but smooth stone. Retracing his steps, he inched around the other side, facing upriver. A ledge projected out three feet from the face of the outcrop. Under the ledge was a small hollowed-out cavity.

Ramsey explored the hole, hopes rising with anticipation. It was sufficient to accommodate his body. Scrabbling over the ground on all fours, he tore up damp grass and gathered leaves. He instinctively covered a wide area, careful not to denude only one spot.

Stuffing all the materials into the hole, he burrowed deep into the nest. Not too bad, he mused, arranging his body into different positions, testing for comfort. Satisfied he had accomplished all that was possible, he closed his eyes and willed the presence of sleep.

Dawn came fully to the river valley. Mist and drizzle still hung in the air, a few hours' respite until the heavy rains began anew. Above Ramsey's sanctuary a narrow road paralleled the passage of the river. In fact the road ran all the way to the sea, connecting the hamlets dotting its path with the major north-south highway.

Ramsey was halfway home on his journey to the sea. He did not, of course, realize the progress he had made. There were still many obstacles to his odyssey. Several hamlets stood in his path. A major bridge, recently bombed and under repair by hundreds of conscripted workers, spanned his river.

For the moment none of this meant anything to the sleeping man. Deep, dreamless oblivion blessed his rest. The river rolled on to the sea as it had done for all of man's existence on the planet.

Traffic began to move down the road, headed for the market center located by the bridge. Farmers, bringing what little they had to sell in exchange for small luxuries. They were generally old, shuffling alongside carts, their conical hats obscuring ancient faces.

Now and then an army truck roared down the road. Young soldiers sat in the rear, arrogant with their importance as liberators and warriors. Peasants scurried to the side of the road in response to the blaring horns of the trucks.

The road noise penetrated Ramsey's dark unconscious void. He jerked awake, instantly alert, weighing the possible dangers. He evaluated his position in relation to the road and knew he could not be detected by the traffic. But he would have difficulty moving around freely.

He needed food to ease the sharp, growing pains in his stomach. He tried to sleep again, relaxing his muscles one by one. Sometime later he awoke to engine noise. A small truck, followed by a squad of local militia, advanced slowly down the road.

They were looking for him, he knew it immediately. From his position he caught brief glimpses of the truck as it grounded leisurely by in first gear. Tran stood in the rear, scanning the road on either side. Oahn walked down the center of the road directing the militiamen.

Ramsey burrowed deeper into his cave, chuckling softly. Tran must be goin' out of his skull. No way in hell he could cover all the jungle from here to the coast. Tran was probably hoping for a bloated corpse washed up by the river bank. Something to show his superiors as evidence, indicating the futility of escape from his camp.

Well, reflected Ramsey, he might just get his fuckin' body if I don't get something to eat soon. The truck growled off in the distance, the troops moving no more than five or ten feet into the jungle on either side of the road. Ramsey felt safer, more confident. He ventured slowly from his hole.

Judging from the strongest source of light penetrating the overcast, it was midmorning. Soon it would begin to rain again. He moved carefully downstream parallel to the river. The foliage was heavy, thick with moisture. He found himself breathing painfully as he forced his way through the clinging vegetation.

He knew it was crazy to be moving around. The original plan was to hide and rest during the day. He was driven, not by hunger, but by the need to feel he was making progress. Also the stimulation of danger. Once again he was pitted against the enemy in a struggle to survive.

Ramsey could still hear the faint receding sound of the truck's engine. He came upon a small clearing, grass-covered and elliptical in shape. Why such an oasis in the middle of the thick rain forest? He had no answer. To his delight, at the far end of the clearing was a stand of stunted banana trees.

The bananas were half the normal size, but the fruit seemed dazzlingly beautiful to the hungry man. Controlling the urge to gorge himself, Ramsey chose two of the larger ones and peeled away the skin. They were hard and relatively tasteless, but appreciated by Ramsey as much as a sumptuous banquet.

He decided to remain near the clearing until dark, eating his fill. The rains began. He took shelter under one of the trees and munched happily, content with his freedom. He was now beginning to feel he could really succeed. The big question remained. What would he do when he got to the sea?

He wondered what retributions his escape would bring down on the other prisoners. There would be reprisals, of that he was sure. Tran would want information even if it was fabricated. The interrogator had to build a defense for himself against the obligatory investigation.

If Swanson and Wilson were lucky, Tran would be replaced. The new man would want his shot at them before he too decided to send them north. Perhaps then his escape would prove to be a blessing, he rationalized. It actually might buy some time for the other prisoners.

The deluge was massive now, rainwater cascading down through the leaves on his unprotected head and shoulders. Ramsey folded one of the larger leaves into a funnel. Catching one of the streams, he directed the water into his mouth. He was physically uncomfortable but mentally eager, ready to begin the journey again.

He was growing impatient. How to occupy his mind? His thoughts strayed to Cathy. The hazy face emerged and vanished. Try as he might, the image would not materialize in any truly recognizable form. The pieces just would not come together. Sad, he thought, a physical pain of remorse and longing heavy in his chest.

Enough, he cautioned. Concentrate, get with it, almost time to go. More bananas, store up for the long night, store up energy. Have to find a log or something to act as a raft. He would give it one more hour. No, use the remaining light to find a suitable log.

Pushing down a last banana, he made his way back to the river bank. It was impossible to move along the edge amid the tangle of brush and roots. He dropped into the water, pushing himself five yards from the edge. Even in the last glimmers of day and the downpour he felt exposed and vulnerable.

Sinking low in the water, he sidestroked downstream, eyes searching the near bank. Almost immediately he felt a tingle from his right ankle trailing over the bottom. He reached down and tore the disgusting blob from his leg before the leech fully imbedded itself in his flesh. He whispered to the night, shivering, "How I hate those slimy bastards."

Through the curtain of rain he spotted a likely-looking branch ensnared by a web of roots. Heaving and straining, he managed to free the log. It would support his weight quite well. Darkness had not fully embraced the river. He would press on anyway. Pushing the branch to midstream, he draped an arm comfortably over his companion.

The river swept in a slow curve to the left. He could not see around the bend. It was too late. He caught the odor before he actually saw the danger. The jungle thinned out dramatically and then came to an abrupt halt at the edge of a low plain a few hundred yards downstream. Set back from the river was a hamlet fronted by paddies adjacent to it.

The smell in the air was a mingling of cooking fires and human fertilizer. Closer now, he caught sounds drifting on the slight breeze blowing off the land. Ramsey unhooked his arm and sank beneath the dark waters. He clung to the underside of the log, holding his breath.

Lungs aching, he surfaced to find the branch drifting toward a canal used to irrigate the paddies during the dry season. Now the canal was full, the river water swirling into its narrow opening. The waterway led in a straight line to the village, paddies on either side.

The last thing he wanted was to go floating down the canal amid the fires glowing in the gathering darkness. He tried to touch bottom but could not. He debated momentarily, then began to swim, dragging the raft with his arm and kicking underwater.

It soon became obvious he was making little headway and exhausting himself in the attempt. Reluctantly he abandoned the log and struck out on his own. Once back in midstream he turned on his back, bobbing gently in the current. The hamlet passed into the night.

On he went, the rain beating on his upturned face, regretting the loss of his second raft. From time to time he flipped over and swam, taking in his surroundings and position relative to the river banks. There was little to see beyond the dark waters. A black curtain draped the world.

Periodically he would detect a flash of light that he interpreted to be distant lightning or perhaps a truck on the road above the river. He was tired, very tired. He decided a brief rest was needed. Once on the bank, he sat shivering in the rain, unable to control his shaking body.

It would be senseless to go floundering around in the thick brush and tall grass now flanking the river. He curled up in a ball, his hands clasped between jumping, quivering thighs. He gave up, back to the river.

It was at least slightly warmer submerged in the muddy water. Ramsey's brain kept sending messages to his eyes telling the lids to close down for the night. Sometimes they obeyed, shutting briefly until he sank beneath the surface. It became a game, to count until he lapsed into a brief unconscious state and then rose like a whale blowing clear his air passages. Up and down like a cork, he was carried on down the river.

The bridge appeared in the distance, a dull glow illuminating the structure. On the approaches hundreds of people tamped and packed the earth. The span itself was swarming with colonies of workers. On a ridge high above the bridge a radar disc lazily scanned the empty sky for aircraft. Carefully hooded lights cast a muted glow over the scene.

The work proceeded at a furious pace. Within twelve hours the damage inflicted by high-flying bombers would be completely repaired. Traffic would flow normally, carrying supplies to the south. Reconnaissance flights would find the structure intact and the cycle would resume again. Bombers would take off from some distant field, drop their payloads, and destroy the bridge.

Ramsey surveyed the scene from his position upstream of the structure. He was amazed. No wonder these people are givin' us a run for our money, he thought. He clung to an overhanging branch and smeared his face and arms heavily with thick, dark mud.

The rain had abated, a thick mist hung over the river. The lights from the bridge shimmered across the surface of the water. His skin might catch the reflection and there he would be, a marshmallow floating on a chocolate-brown surface.

He slowly drifted under the bridge. The chattering of the workers could be heard clearly above the sounds of repair. He wondered what they would think if they knew an American was passing directly under their scurrying feet.

Ramsey clung to one of the bridge supports, secretly enjoying his presence among the enemy. Looking up, he could see shadows flitting back and forth between the gaps in the timbers. He was twenty-five to thirty feet below the actual structure. Finally, almost with reluctance, he released his grip and floated free.

He felt an odd sensation of loss. The thoughts and feelings he was experiencing were disturbing. He realized a curious kinship with the people on the bridge. He knew from his reading that kidnapers or terrorists and their victims sometimes became allied and dependent on each other.

It had something to do with being alone again, isolated from human contact. He drifted away, shaking himself free of such melancholy thoughts, and turned his face downstream. How much longer, he wondered. It can't be far. That bridge must be part of the coastal highway route.

On each side of the river he could detect signs of human habitation. The river was growing wider. The current now meandered slowly back and forth. Lights appeared on both banks, and dimly perceived structures stood out against the dark sky.

Ramsey tried to estimate the time, based on his entry into the river near dusk. Perhaps two or three in the morning was his guess. If he reached the sea tonight, he would try to locate a village near the mouth of the river. If not, it would mean hiding out for another day, and that increased the risk of discovery....

18

THE SEA

THE RAIN had stopped and, much like the previous evening, gaps appeared in the leaden sky. Ramsey knew he didn't have much left. Alarm bells were beginning to sound in his clouded brain. He struggled for clarity, shaking his head to rid the rolling fog behind his eyes.

The river had finished its journey, emptying into the sea. Almost comatose, Ramsey was unaware of his passage. He slipped beneath the surface, willing sleep and peace, the water warm, comforting his tired body. His heart slowed and the systems began to shut down.

From somewhere back in the recess of his being a pulse flashed and exploded. Struggling, fighting his way to the surface, he broke free. He was there. The dream had come to be. The water in his mouth was salty. Ramsey laughed, a hoarse, crackling sound.

He was surrounded by turbulence. The river, meeting the oncoming sea, kicked up small waves. Ramsey's numbed senses began to function as he was repeatedly slapped in the face. He was laughing, gagging, and choking in a spontaneous display of joy.

He was slowly floating seaward. No good, he thought, a few hours and he would be shark bait. His tired body reluctantly responded and he pushed for the shore. Almost instinctively he had headed for the land on the southern edge of the river.

Approaching the dark outline of the shore, his heart lifted with elation. It was there just as he had imagined and planned. He discerned the shapes of numerous hooches huddled along the shoreline. Treading water, he rose and fell in motion with the light surf.

There was no sign of activity, no smoke, no lights. Why should there be? he considered. I'm the only asshole swimmin' around in the middle of the night. Still, he knew extreme caution was necessary; it could all end right here.

Fishermen, by habit, rose before the rest of mankind. It had to be a fishing community. It had to be, he sent up a silent plea. Why else would they have settled here, by the edge of the sea?

Drifting closer, he could distinguish many elongated shapes drawn up on the beach. Boats, he almost screamed aloud in his excitement. The Big Guy in the sky is takin' care of this sorry-ass boonie rat tonight. A low, subdued chuckle. Exhaustion and aching limbs forgotten.

His feet scraped the bottom. Ramsey waded in, the sea tugging gently on his legs. The water grew shallow, circling his knees. He got down on his belly and pulled forward until his upper body lay on the beach. He listened intently, the water foaming around his prostrate body.

Ramsey low-crawled through the sand, pausing to listen every few feet. The evening was tranquil, disturbed only by the gentle ocean sounds. A harsh, wracking cough from one of the nearby huts halted his progress. Once again, breathing normally, he continued until he lay between two of the boats.

The craft were wooden, about fourteen feet in length. Ramsey knelt and peered inside one of the boats. The high, square stern had a deep notch where, Ramsey guessed, some type of tiller would be mounted. There was a single seat across the stern for a helmsman. The gunwales curved to a sharply pointed bow.

Then the most useful discovery of all. A mast, with sail furled, lay in the bottom of the boat. Near the bow Ramsey could see where the mast was stepped. Alongside the mast was a single broad oar. He assumed this was a combination tiller and paddle.

Here was all he could possibly hope for to complete his journey. Now all he had to do was get the boat into the water without being detected. He thought of scrounging around for food but decided the risk was too great.

Fishermen must use nets. Where the hell are the nets? he wondered. With nets he could conceivably catch fish and sustain himself on the voyage south. He squirmed forward beyond the boats. What would you do with nets at the end of a day's fishing? Hang the suckers up to dry, of course, numbnuts. He had to get out of this habit, talking to himself. No good. But what the fuck, at least he could hold an intelligent conversation.

There they were, by Jesus, draped over a frame shaped like a soccer goal. They were casting nets, not very big, weighted at one end. One man could handle the whole operation. Find a school of fish, cast the net, allow it to sink, then haul it in, spilling the contents into the bottom of the boat.

He had to pull in the reins. The euphoric imaginings were a creation of his tired brain. He was like a diver experiencing nitrogen narcosis. Nothing mattered, he had it made. Boat, sail, everything. Nothing could stop him now.

He shook his head violently from side to side until

pinpoints of light danced before his eyes. Fuck you, Ramsey, fuck you, he screamed inside his head. Get with it. Couple-a-hundred miles above the DMZ and you figure you got it made. Shape up, asshole, get with the program!

A door banged shut and a dim figure shuffled from one of the huts. Ramsey pressed his body into the cold sand, watching the intruder. The man stopped five feet away from the hooch and reached inside his nightclothes. Ramsey could see steam rising from the stream of urine as it contacted the cool night air and splashed on the ground. The man stretched his arms to the sky before returning to his hut.

That did it. Ramsey was wide awake, biting his lips, digging fingernails into palms, curling toes, anything to activate his sluggish body. Come too far to lose it all, he admonished his fuzzy brain.

Separating the nets, he pulled one from the frame and deposited it carefully in the bottom of a boat. Now came the test. Could he actually drag the boat to the sea? The sand was at least reasonably firm.

Well, here we go. He bunched the tired muscles and heaved on the bow. An inch or so, that was all. Again, not much. Straining, he pulled, thin, taut sinews jumping and quivering. He gained a foot, no more.

He let loose with a stream of silent curses aimed at the tumbling, boiling clouds. He could do nothing more. Kneeling beside the bow, he tried to swallow his anger. To have come this far, twenty feet from the fuckin' ocean. Tears of frustration rolled down the filthy face.

He remained crouched for fully ten minutes. Finally his self-pity gave way to an attitude of detached calm. He had a problem and sure as hell couldn't solve it by cryin' like a friggin' baby. Think, he told himself.

How did they get the boats into the water? There must be a way. He crawled back to the stern and searched the dark sand. Nothing. He moved back to the hanging nets. There it was, underneath the nets, a round smooth log. Simple, shit, I should have known it, he admonished.

He rolled the log down the beach to the bow of his boat. He had actually begun to think of the craft in possessive terms. Standing, he heaved on the bow and with his foot pushed the roller into position. Straining again, he inserted the log further under the hull.

Now he was ready. After a brief rest, he pulled the boat forward until the stern dropped off the roller, a dull thud, hitting the soft sand. A second repetition had the bow in the water. One more time and he was long gone. The boat was afloat, ready for the sea.

A final glance at the river and distant dark hills. He pushed into deeper water. Using the oar, he continued until he could no longer touch bottom. He went forward to the bow and now used the oar as a paddle.

The sky over the sea had less cloud cover. Light filtered down and illuminated long, rolling swells of the deeper water. He was half a mile from shore. A slight breeze was blowing straight off the land. Not exactly what he wanted, it would mean tacking to stay close inshore.

Time to raise the sail. He dropped the mast into the hole cut through a board stretched across the beam of the boat near the bow. The sail was a triangular lateen made of heavy cloth. Loops of the same material slid along a primitive bamboo boom. There was a rope circle secured near the base of the mast. By experimentation Ramsey found that if he doubled the circle over, the boom fit securely through the rope.

A line running through a notch at the masthead allowed him to raise the sail. He secured it in place by tying the line on the forward edge of the boom. He was not quite sure if his improvisation was the original design, but it seemed to make sense. Certainly not a craft for blue-water sailing or a heavy blow; however, it would move. That was all he cared about.

By using the oar as a tiller and controlling the sail by a single line leading aft, he headed out for the distant horizon. Ramsey had no desire to be in open water when the sun rose. His plan was to sail at night and find someplace along the shore to hide during daylight.

The theft of the boat would surely initiate a search. He knew the naval capability of the enemy was virtually nonexistent, but they must possess some kind of patrol craft that could be called into service, he reasoned. At least for the first few days he must contain himself and stick to the plan. He cautioned, patience, patience....

19

THE SPIT

HE FELT totally at ease gliding over the calm sea. The little boat was making about three knots, he figured, trailing a hand in the water. The tiller, awkward at first, seemed to function quite well once he had solved its eccentricities.

He was soon able to sit in the bottom of the boat and allow the craft virtually to sail itself. He was headed slightly southeast, but too far to seaward. Trying for a more southerly course, he pushed the oar over until the sail began flapping. Back on the tiller, satisfied he was making all headway possible, he began to plan ahead.

He was exhausted. He knew it would be impossible to keep going much longer. Judging from the sky conditions, dawn was not far away. Another fifteen minutes on this tack and he would head for shore. The problem was to find an isolated stretch of coast. Again, he would depend on his luck to pull him through.

He wished the coming day was over and he could sail a whole night. He would fish along the way and put distance between himself and the enemy. In the meantime he had to stay hidden, assuming he would probably end up no more than three miles south of the river mouth.

Coming about, he headed for the dark bulk of the land. He noticed with satisfaction that a current parallel to the shore was aiding his southerly drift. The swish of the ocean around the hull was hypnotic. Night sailing had always been his favorite. But now he was having difficulty keeping his eyes open.

He reached over the side and splashed seawater over his face and neck. In a further effort to remain alert he stood, bracing against the gentle motion of the boat. He was now about a mile offshore. The timing was all-important. To arrive in semidarkness and not be able to fully reconnoiter the surroundings was dangerous, but more so would be a daylight landing.

To the south he saw a finger of land reaching out to seaward. This would be his destination. The spit of land appeared too narrow for any type of settlement. He approached cautiously, dropping the sail and taking up the paddle.

On the northern side was a curving, sandy beach. Ramsey decided to investigate the southern flank before attempting to land. Dipping the oar quietly, he rounded the point of the spit. Heavy vegetation to the water's edge stretched as far as he could see along the inward curve of the land.

Coasting along the shore, he could see in the now gray light the possibilities of concealment. There was a strip of sand no more than five feet wide. The small beach was overhung in many spots, branches and vines trailing in the sand.

Time to hit the beach, Ramsey decided, turning the bow toward the land. Halfway down the point, the boat ground on the beach. Before trying to hide, he resolved to explore in both directions. Retreating into the water to avoid leaving tracks, he waded toward the mainland.

He could detect no sign of life on the finger of land. Near the end where the land began to turn southward he paused, tuning in to the sounds of dawn. Nothing unfamiliar.

Then, as he turned to retrace his steps, distant engine noise carried down by the wind caused his stomach to churn. It could be Tran and his boys, still searching. The terrain, which had always been in favor of the enemy, was now his ally.

The road was hidden, a good half mile from the ocean. If indeed it was a search party, he doubted they would venture down through the thick jungle to scour the beach. His more present danger lay to the sea. A passing fisherman might spot him and report his whereabouts.

Time to get rollin' and dig in for the night, he resolved, feeling confident that the open-water end of the spit held nothing of interest. Returning to the boat, he positioned the bow opposite a dark cave created by overhanging foliage.

Pushing from the stern, Ramsey managed to slide half the length under the green curtain. He had profited from his earlier experience. Using the boom as a roller, he slowly inched the boat under cover. As a further precaution, he piled leaves and brush along the hull. He made adjustments of the camouflage, returning to the water and viewing the area from all angles. Finally satisfied, he used a switch of brush to eradicate his footprints and backed in under the umbrella of vegetation.

It was fully daylight by the time he was through. He lay down beside the boat. Mist and drizzle hung monotonously in the air. Since he had not been dry for days, the damp and dripping sanctuary did not really disturb him.

How would he spend the long day? Two main

objectives to be accomplished: sleep and food. For now he was content simply to rest and contemplate his time of freedom. He had been incredibly lucky, all the elements of his plan had fallen into place.

Of course the biggest factor contributing to his success was that he had done the unexpected. To escape from the North and make your way through enemy territory, where you stood out rather obviously, was an almost unheard-of achievement. The sea was his friend, balancing the odds somewhat evenly.

The crisscross of leaves and vines above his head, viewed through half-closed eyes, faded into blackness and he slept. The world around him came awake and began to function in its natural cycle, unperturbed by his presence. Traffic increased on the vital coastal road above the sea. Fishing boats strung out across the horizon. Larger motorized craft moved offshore. Smaller boats powered by various means clung nearer the land.

The day was typically overcast, light fog shrouded the sea and coastal plain. The ocean was dark and brooding under the leaden sky. From the spit the land curved gently in and then seaward again, forming a large peninsula obscuring the coast to the south. Beyond, the coastline was uniform, broken only by the entrance to the sea of the Bang Hieng River.

The river estuary was straddled by a major settlement. Fifty miles beyond the river was Ramsey's goal, the imaginary line dividing North and South. The impending adversities against which the slumbering man would be pitted awaited his approach with indifference. The sea, the enemy, both equally lethal, were for the moment forgotten. His mind rambled among deep niches of the past.

Eyelids twitching and fluttering, Ramsey tried to slow the blur of faces whirling through his mind. A spinning carousel of mirrors flashed the images behind his eyes. Faces superimposed on faces. Smiles and tears, anguish and laughter, swept by in milliseconds, then vanished, receding into blinding light.

He jerked in his sleep, struggling to focus and slow the parade of his past. There was Cathy, face lined with sadness, gone, replaced by a vision of death, a dying comrade. His father's frowning countenance appeared, only to fade as Swanson, head thrown back in laughter, slipped over the shining screen.

Davidson's death mask, Tran screaming obscenities, lips curling back, teeth bared. Guards' faces animated in staccato conversation. The volume of their exchange grew louder and more insistent. Ramsey's body convulsed, the words penetrating his sluggish brain.

His eyes flew open. The words were all around, seeping into the green sanctuary. He lay rigid, listening, processing the sounds. Two, three different voices chattering, laughing, exchanging insults. A search party was his first thought. But then he considered, why broadcast their position and presence with such lack of stealth? Perhaps to flush him out into the guns of some secreted force. Was this the solution to the commotion?

He slowed his rapid breathing and tried to locate the direction of the voices. Neither to his left nor right, but forward, out over the water. A patrol boat, no it couldn't be, he thought, it's too shallow in the protected bay.

He elbowed his way forward through the grass, keeping to the shadows cast by the awning of trees. Through a narrow opening in the hanging foliage he saw three boats. They were ranged across the mouth of the bay. The nearest was no more than twenty-five yards away.

In each boat a man stood casting his net into the midst of a churning school of small silver fish. The multicolor hulls dipped and bobbed with each heave and retrieval of the nets. The fishermen were obviously enjoying their good fortune. Their shouts and laughter resounded across the water. They compared catches and exaggerated the size of each haul.

Behind the boats, in deep water, large menacing shapes swept back and forth gorging on the fleeing school. Between the larger predators and the boats, the little fish had no choice but to crowd into the bay. They were easy prey.

Ramsey comprehended the situation immediately and relaxed, viewing the events dispassionately. The panicked fish milled closer and closer to the shore. It occurred to Ramsey that the situation might well prove to be beneficial rather than threatening.

More and more of the tiny fish were hurling themselves on the beach not ten feet from his hiding place. The fishing boats drew closer. Ramsey slipped back into the dark recesses of his jungle cave. He lay listening to the excited cries of the fishermen and prayed they would soon have their fill. He surmised they would not want to be at sea when the heavy late-afternoon wind and rains arrived.

Perhaps it was wishful dreaming on his part, but he could not imagine the men landing to collect the stranded fish. Those tiny bodies that he had come to covet would, it was hoped, be considered excess victims of the battle and left to other scavengers. As if on cue, the whir of wings and harsh screeches filled the air and descended on the beach.

Sea birds wheeled and dove into the carnage, flipping the tiny fish headfirst down their gullets. Ramsey beat his fists on the ground in frustration. "You bastards, you rotten thieving bastards," he spat at the whirling birds. Desperate, he crawled forward, pausing at the last cover before the sand.

The boats, low in the water, weighted down with their catch, were making for the end of the point. The fishermen strained at the oars, seeking the open sea and wind. The rowers were still facing his hiding place. Ramsey could only watch with anguished eyes as the birds consumed the remnants of the fish.

At last, sails raised, the boats disappeared from

view. Leaping to his feet, Ramsey charged onto the beach, arms flapping like some deranged soul. The feeding birds rose reluctantly before this strange apparition. He scrambled along the beach gathering slippery carcasses, some with gills still quivering.

They slipped through his grasping fingers like quicksilver. He could hold no more than two or three at a time. Anger welled up in his throat; he ran back to the boat and threw his meager catch into the bottom. Pulling his tattered shirt over his head, he returned to the beach.

Quickly he spread the torn fabric on the sand and threw the remaining fish within his reach in its general direction. The birds had enough of this intruder. They dove within inches of his head, beating about his shoulders. He flailed about, the air filled with screaming furies. Talons raked across his vulnerable back bent to gather in a silver shape with vacant eye.

He could not defend himself from the swarming throng. He gathered his makeshift bundle and sought the haven of the trees. The mocking cries followed him beneath his shroud of greenery.

His back throbbed. The red lines gouged across his spine oozed and bubbled. Ignoring the pain, he clambered into the boat and spilled his bundle onto the bottom planks. Greedily he gloated over his catch. Twelve tiny fish lay amidst the grime accumulated in the depths of the hull.

They reminded him of smelt, caught as a boy.

Long, shaky floats stretching out over gray water. Breath misting, frozen fingers jerking the pole. A long time ago, buddy, he thought sadly. Cleaned and cooked in butter, delicious, I'm all set, no problem. All I need is a knife, butter, and a frypan.

Despair, like the shadowy murk, crept in on the edges of his mind. He looked at the tiny bodies with baleful eyes. Well, I can make like a sea gull and flip them in, or chew 'em like a French fry. He mulled over his alternatives. He knew he was about to eat the fish; his stomach craved sustenance. How to go about it was the problem.

He selected one of the fish and carefully wiped away the grains of sand clinging to the silver-green scales. The liquid dead eye returned his stare. "The hell with it," he voiced his decision to the unblinking eye.

Grimacing, he bit off half the body and forced himself to chew rapidly. He crunched the whole mess together in his mouth. Small bones, skin, and guts congealed into a soggy, evil-tasting blob. He gulped and swallowed with closed eyes.

He gagged but continued stoically to consume the fish. He reasoned nothing much worse could happen to his body. By the time he was chewing on his seventh morsel, the taste and texture of his meal made little impression. The shrunken stomach actually felt satisfied when he had finished.

He knew the feeling wouldn't last. He decided to

sweep the area in hopes of dessert and supplies for the coming night. The spit was perhaps thirty yards across. To the landward end the foliage was dense and thickly tangled. His progress was extremely slow as he traversed the point.

He found some white tubers reaching above the soil. Digging down, he found a pulpy white vegetable. It had a nondescript taste, much like a potato. Ramsey gathered in his harvest and with the tubers returned to the boat.

On the seaward end of the spit he found nothing of value. Sounds of small animals scurrying from his path did not arouse his interest. Even if he were able to capture them, the idea of eating raw rodent flesh was repulsive.

Retracing his path, an alien sound immobilized him, rigid in place. He identified the sound immediately, the low rumbling throb of a diesel. The engine was turning slowly, approaching the northern side of the point.

The boat was moving inshore, coming closer. Fighting down the urge to run for his hiding place, Ramsey dropped to his belly. Slowly he crawled over roots and beneath the low brush, hugging the ground. He heard shouted commands aboard the craft. The pitch of the engine dropped.

Ramsey could not see the ocean from his concealed position. He could, however, guess at the intent of whatever craft was closing in on the point. The crawl back to his boat seemed endless. After several detours around heavy brush and thorns, he reached the hidden clearing. Breathing harshly, he checked the improvised camouflage. Satisfied, he crawled forward behind a banyan tree.

The entire length of the point was visible. Rain had begun to splatter and dimple the surface of the water, making it difficult to detect the movement of the intruding craft. The burgeoning downpour muffled the engine sound.

Ramsey involuntarily drew within himself, hunching back. The bow of the boat swung into view. It resembled the old PT boats he had seen in World War II movies. The craft turned. Ramsey could see a man standing in the bow scanning the shoreline with binoculars.

The man swiveled his head and shouted an order to the helmsman. The boat backed down into deeper water. Behind the man whom Ramsey assumed to be the skipper, a mounted .50 caliber machine gun traversed ominously, covering the beach.

Another shouted order carried on the wind. The gunner opened up, spraying a section of brush opposite the boat. The heavy chatter of the gun startled Ramsey. The ripping tearing of rounds through the vegetation caused him to cling even closer to the ground.

They can't know I'm here, he reasoned. They're tryin' to spook me, flush me into running. He shivered, clutching the roots and base of the tree even tighter. The sound of spent rounds striking the deck reverberated across the water.

The firing ceased. The gunner had consumed a whole belt of ammunition. In spite of the driving rain and chill wind, sweat erupted across Ramsey's forehead. The thin line of the bow swung back and forth, coming closer. Ramsey could make out the details of the captain's face. He was small, chunky, with close-cropped hair.

Don't let it end here, prayed Ramsey, blown away like some fuckin' reptile clingin' to the earth. He held his breath as the lenses of the binoculars steadied and appeared to be focused directly on his eyes. The man was staring into his soul, sucking out his life force and the possibility of freedom.

An abrupt movement, the glasses lowered, a gesture to the gunner or perhaps the helmsman. Ramsey closed his eyes against the terrible impact of the heavy slugs. Every muscle tensed, awaiting the singing death about to sweep across the point.

The boat picked up speed, propeller biting into the water. The stern was partially visible, indicating a turn to port. The patrol craft, its wake now reaching out to Ramsey, headed south.

Ramsey buried his face in the damp earth. Instead of relief, he experienced a keen, stabbing pain of despair. How much more of this could be endured? Physically he was growing more feeble with each passing hour. The up and down jerks of intense emotion had taken a toll on his mental capacities. He was truly a man on the brink, poised between light and darkness. He gave in and slept, not moving, curled behind the banyan tree.

The rain continued driving, obliterating all sounds except the soft slap of the ocean at the edge of the land. Darkness came swiftly, cascading down from the highland ridges. Overhead, huge bombers thundered across the night sky unmolested in their journey north.

Their crews by morning would be asleep in comfortable safe quarters far from the devastation they had wrought. Far at sea a carrier retrieved a flight of planes returning from a napalm strike on a suspected N.V.A. encampment. To the south, defensive positions were dug, strengthened, prepared for the long night belonging to the enemy.

Ramsey slept on undisturbed, a small microcosm caught up in the huge whirling vortex of war. Great scudding clouds whipped down off the mountains. The torrential rain battered across the point. His sleep was deep and profound.

Then they came, the scavengers. Pinpoints of fire and pain stunned his brain. They were all over his half-naked body, sand crabs clawing and pinching. The edge of the beach was black with their scuttling bodies. The clicking of their claws and legs filled the air with unholy racket.

Ramsey sprang to his feet screaming, shaking himself violently. They fell from his body but swarmed around his legs seeking flesh. He made a series of leaps back in the direction of the boat. The crabs, wary of entering the jungle, did not follow.

What else? he thought. Birds, leeches, and crabs; it's me against the whole fuckin' animal kingdom. Hold on, buddy—the idea pushed back his self-pity—I can eat those bastards. Back to the edge of the beach, he grabbed two behind their claws. They reached back over their bodies but couldn't reach his hand.

Chuckling to himself, he smashed them down onto the bottom planks of the boat. He made several more trips, each time relishing the violent act of crushing the bodies against the wood. He was fighting back against the environment that had manipulated his destiny.

Gratified, he began to prepare for the night's voyage. The brush was set aside, the boat swung around facing the ocean. He stored his provisions up near the bow and checked the mast and lines. The rain still fell, but with less intensity. Wind rising up over the highlands pushed down over the coastal plain to the southeast. This was precisely the direction of his voyage to freedom.

Confidence restored, Ramsey inched the boat from under the now dark protective awning. It took fifteen minutes of grunting and straining before the hull rested in the water. The ocean was warm swirling around his cold, cramped body. He pushed into deeper water.

Scrambling aboard, he paddled down the length

of the point, striving for the open sea. The wind was already pushing the craft south. The sail billowed and snapped taut in the breeze. The boat immediately surged forward, embraced by the wind.

"Baby," he exulted, "if this wind holds, I'm goin' to make some miles tonight." His spirit soared as the little boat cut through the water. Ramsey tossed a stray palm leaf over the side and watched it slip rapidly by the hull. It was soon lost in the frothing wake....

20
THE ENEMY

FOUR AND a half, five knots, he speculated. Given ten hours of uninterrupted sailing, he could put forty miles under the keel. The surface of the sea was slightly illuminated by phosphorescence. A thin dividing line existed between the sea and the inky blackness of the sky.

Small curling waves pushed against the boat's stern. The sail, out over the port side, was catching the wind beautifully. The wake was straight, very little adjustment necessary. Ramsey merely rested the tiller under his arm and propped his feet along the gunwale.

Far to his right, inland, feathers of light flared across the dark underbellies of the clouds. A B-52 strike or lightning, he thought, feeling oddly detached from the whole scene. Seconds later, muffled, distinctive crumps were borne on the wind. It had been a bombing mission.

Shit, time for my evening repast. Garçon, table for one, he chuckled. Leaving the tiller to its own swaying motion through the water, he reached for two crushed crab bodies. He broke the claws and legs from the carcasses, which he tossed over the side.

Sucking out the juices and slippery meat, he felt infinitely pleased with himself. He had been tested mightily and judged himself not wanting. Absorbing the sea and wind sounds, he savored the watery, salty meat. He was caught up, emotionally captured by the aura of the open sea. Freedom, once again freedom, one forever with the ocean. A deceitful euphoria that nothing could touch him out here on the breast of eternity.

His mind strayed to a time off Nantucket. He had been sailing the coast with the family of a friend from school. Up and down Long Island Sound, basking in the simple days of summer. Now a final sortie out into the Atlantic, before heading back to Boston.

They had sailed all night, involved with the peace and tranquillity of a smooth, following sea. Around dawn the wind died and the sloop lay dead in the water. The boat wallowed, rolling with the long undulating swell. The sun charged violent red above the horizon, sending shafts of fire across the sea of glass.

They were about to start the engine and shatter the morning calm. Strange whooshing sounds wafted across the crimson sea. Great leviathans rose and breached, sending sprays of vapor high into the still air. They were all around the boat, the nearest less than a hundred feet away.

The whales were accompanied by groups of dolphins. The playful, grinning creatures approached and dove under and around the sloop. The sight was awesome and inspiring. Huge scarred heads broke the surface and rolled under the placid sea. One whale sounded, the enormous tail raised high, then slammed down, white water boiling high in the air. The sound thundered across the water.

For more than an hour the great beasts cavorted around the tiny sloop. They seemed to sense the human presence, and like their smaller brothers, the dolphins, decided to entertain the visitors to their domain. The only element of fear to the display was that a careless whale might surface under the boat and stove in the hull. It had been known to happen, but with angry or sick whales, not like these frolicking inhabitants of the deep.

Then they were gone, resuming an instinctual course to some far mating or feeding ground. Nothing remained to evidence their passing. The sea was flat, unbroken and serene.

The wind had abated slightly, but Ramsey still made good speed through the water. The breeze carried muted engine noise from the coastal road out over the sea. There were no visible lights, but Ramsey knew from experience that the whole country moved at night, using the darkness as a shield.

No amount of bombing would stem the flow of supplies to the south. The small boat ghosted along, Ramsey dozing for minutes at a time. It was during one of these brief reposes that he was jolted awake by a sharp blow to the middle of his back.

Confused, he swung his head back and forth, seeking his attacker. He located the source of his bewilderment flapping and gasping on the bottom planks. A flying fish had propelled itself over the stern and was halted in midflight by Ramsey's body.

He laughed quietly to himself, dispelling the nervousness. He resolved to keep a more vigilant watch. Stretching, he chose one of the soggy potatoes, or whatever they were, and munched on the tasteless vegetable. To occupy himself he thought of the future and what it might bring. He no longer doubted his ability to escape. It was, simply, only a question of time.

His thoughts then were beyond, focused on the return home. He would become a civilian. Enough of war and the military. He had no wish to be ground up by the machine. A new life, but moving in what direction? he pondered. Go back to school, a career perhaps, even a wife and family.

The thought "wife" immediately provoked images of Cathy. Would it be possible, or was the void too deep? He resolved to try, the attempt had to be made. If nothing came of it, move on with at least a final end, a door closing on a segment of his life.

The boat was approximately three-quarters of a mile offshore. The visibility had increased and the rain became a slight drizzle. Ramsey was cold and cramped, with no way of improving his lot.

Out of the mist ahead rose buildings—not crude huts, but large square structures. He blinked to clear his vision. Sure enough, there it was, a major population center. Hastily adjusting the sail, he changed course as much as the wind would allow. Christ, he thought, I've got to be well past this place before dawn.

He searched through his mind, constructing a map of the North above the DMZ. There were numerous possibilities, Ba Don, Dong Hoi, or Vinh Linh, all strung out along the coast. Ramsey could detect a few flickering lights, but the majority of the city was in darkness. Which one was it? he wondered. If it was Vinh Linh he was close, very close, to the DMZ and freedom.

As he drew closer, the outline of the city became clear. A wide black area divided the buildings into two groupings. Then it became obvious—a river, of course.

Where else for a large settlement? Both Ba Don and Dong Hoi were situated on rivers. He wasn't sure about Vinh Linh; he thought not.

He was headed out, but not quickly or far enough for his peace of mind. He trimmed the sail, catching all he could from the breeze. He was about opposite the harbor entrance. Two large motorized junks negotiated the last bend in the river, making for the reach of harbor and open sea.

Ramsey spotted them almost immediately, their lanterns winking through the night. If he continued on his present course, the boat would pass directly across their bows. He scrambled forward, dropping the sail at the same time. He heaved the mast up and out, lowering it, and himself, to the floorboards.

If he could provide a low silhouette, chances were they would pass him by, missing the dark hull wallowing low in the water. Only his eyes peering over the gunwale, he watched the progress of the junks. At this distance he could see no figures visible on deck, only the swinging lanterns dappling the black sea surface.

He chewed nervously on a tuber. He wondered what they carried, where they were bound. His stomach clutched. They had changed heading and were moving ponderously toward his boat. They would pass thirty or forty yards to seaward. If the boat were spotted, they would certainly investigate.

He played out the scene in his mind. An emaciated man dragged from his hiding place and taken aboard the junk. Trussed up, ropes around his biceps, thrown down into some stinking hold. The man would be forgotten while they were out at sea.

The junks would put in at some port farther up the coast and he would be turned over to the local authorities. There would be confusion and he would be dragged from place to place. Eventually they would discover his identity and he would be sent, not to the old camp, but to Hanoi.

They would make an example of him, show other prisoners and the world this fool who thought he could escape. He pressed his forehead against the rough wood of the hull. No, he resolved, that was not how it would be, never, never again.

If the boat was discovered, he would slip over the side. From there he knew not what, swim to shore, out to sea, however he was moved in the last extremity. He knew if he were taken again he would not be able to resist completely, not after all he had been through.

He would give little bits at a time, and in the process die a fraction each day. It was impossible, wallowing in your own shit and vomit, bound in excruciating positions, to retain much dignity. The enemy did not care. You were a piece of meat, subhuman, to be digested by the bloody maw of war.

The vague silhouettes of the junks moved even closer. He could actually smell them now, a blend of fish and hot cooking oil drifting across water. Voices raised in laughter mocked the shivering, isolated man.

The first junk was now opposite the boat, throbbing beat of the engine loud and threatening. Canvas stretched across the main beam sheltered the crew enjoying an early breakfast. The helmsman traded insults with them.

Ramsey was fascinated. He knew protruding his head above the gunwale was foolish, but still he persisted. As the junk slid by, he continued to watch these men of the sea unperturbed by questions of war or freedom. Their only concern would be for the moment and completion of the voyage.

One down, one to go, he thought, the stern light of the first boat fading rapidly in the overcast. A crewman stood smoking at the rail of the second junk. This is it, sighed Ramsey, sure he would be discovered. The man seemed to be looking directly at the boat. He straightened, flipped his cigarette in a curving arc toward Ramsey, turned on his heel, and vanished.

The junk was gone, consumed by billowing haze and fog. The wind had dropped and the overcast thickened. Ramsey fought back the urge to grab his oar and paddle like a wild man, away from this hostile river mouth.

Dawn was coming. He must find some refuge or take his chance on the sea. There was no wind. He would never be able to get far enough out on the open ocean to be safe. There it was, hole up for another day, that was his only choice.

The decision made, he took up the paddle and began to stroke methodically, ignoring his aching muscles. At least the activity warmed him. He dug and pulled, heading south. The fog lay thick on the surface of the sea. He could not make out the buildings or harbor entrance. His course was blind, dead-reckoned from his last glimpse of the city.

He guessed an hour or so until daylight. The fog would then slowly dissipate. The tidal bore in the river had swung and was now incoming. Ramsey and his boat were carried into the river mouth even as he struggled south.

He paddled through the silent gray world, unaware of his predicament. A shroud had been thrown over the dark, oily sea. He could see no more than fifteen feet beyond the bow. His wrists and shoulders screamed their agony as he tried to maintain the rhythmic stroking.

He rested a moment, chewing mechanically on the remaining vegetable. He listened carefully, motionless in the bow. The distant clanking of machinery and a car horn blaring were the only sounds penetrating the curtain of fog. He could not be sure from which direction the sounds originated. His position in relation to the river and shore remained a mystery.

I could be goin' round and round in circles, he thought. Shrugging his shoulders in a gesture of helplessness and resignation, he began to paddle again. He felt like some primitive man near the dawn of time, confused and frightened by unexplored, dangerous territory.

Ramsey made a silent resolution to himself. If he survived this coming day, he would head straight out to sea when darkness fell. No more of this coast crap, he vowed, too many reminders, the smell, the sounds, everything indicative of enemy presence.

On he paddled through the gray swirling vapor, a spectre... the ferryman on the journey between the living and the dead. His mind lapsed into fantasy. He imagined the far shore was actually rising into view, large pillars looming out of the mist, advancing on the boat. Before he could comprehend, the boat glided between the towering giants.

Ramsey paused in midstroke, clutching for strands of reality. Now he was fully cognizant of his passage. He had drifted under a wharf reaching out into the river. His struggle against the current had been futile.

The boat bumped gently against a growth-encrusted timber. Ramsey circled an arm around the rough wood, maintaining his position against the current. He peered ahead and could see pairs of tall pilings retreating into the gloom.

For lack of a better course of action, he decided to explore the passage guarded by the silent sentinels. In small pockets of clear air he was able to see the dock itself, passing above his head. Then the structure would vanish, obscured, leaving him to grope blindly onward.

His head struck a crossbeam. Gasping with pain, he was thrown sprawling to the floorboards. Dazed, he lay in the bottom. The prow nudged the mud of the river bank and came to a halt. His little boat had successfully navigated the length of the wharf and now lay grounded in the ooze bordering the river.

Ramsey could not sit. He had to double at the waist, there being no more than three and a half feet clearance. He shook himself and rolled over the side into calf-deep water. He slopped his way around the stern and pushed the craft farther into the embankment, then clambered back over the gunwale and arranged himself as comfortably as possible. Trusting his fate to the gods, he closed his eyes.

He was awakened by a number of vivid sensations. First were the rats scurrying about his boat, consuming every remaining morsel of food. Dust sifted from the rough boards overhead. Laden carts rumbled down the length of the dock. Their goal was a large black hull drawn up at the head of the wharf. He could distinguish the shape of the junk clearly because of the striking clarity of the morning.

The sun shone, a minor miracle of sorts during this season of wet. All the world seemed to be in movement with the exception of Ramsey. The black hull rose and fell as river traffic made the roads to the sea. Overhead, voices were raised in argument, the drivers seeking position to off-load.

He cowered, listening to the passage of humanity going about the daily business of life. Hidden deep in the shadows, he could only observe a small portion of the river surrounding the wharf. His view was obstructed by the overhanging timbers of the dock itself.

He could, however, hear the sounds of a busy seaport.

Engines coughed and spluttered, chains rattled, and all about him the voices of the enemy. Oh God, he sighed, I do have an immense talent for landin' myself in crap lately. The dock was about two hundred feet long and some thirty feet wide. Ramsey's boat rested midway across the width against the gently sloping embankment.

He considered moving to either side. This would afford a full view of the river and the port. He decided to remain where he was until the junk was loaded and the activity overhead ceased. Carts continued to rumble down the length of the dock. The slow plodding of animal hoofs echoed out over the river. Occasionally a light truck joined the parade. Convinced he was safe from detection in the dark recess of the dock, he tried to sleep. He was too tense; the proximity of other humans would not allow him to relax.

The aroma of cooking permeating the light breeze kindled with a vengeance his need for food. There was little chance of obtaining any kind of satisfaction from his present surroundings. The brown river would surely yield nothing, and the muddy embankment was, likewise, a dim prospect. Ramsey considered stringing his yet unused net in hopes of snaring a creature of some type. The evidence floating by, consisting of garbage and human waste, cancelled that idea.

21
EBB TIDE

HIS REVERIE ended abruptly. Movement to the right caught his attention. A small pair of brown legs was visible from the knees down. They were, however, increasing in length as the child descended, headed for the water's edge.

The boy, clad only in black shorts, bent and slapped the surface of the water with a short flat stick. The child only had to turn his head to the left, peer under the wharf, and Ramsey would be discovered.

The boy continued to amuse himself, splashing and laughing.

Ramsey hardly breathed. He sat hunched over in the boat, totally motionless, watching the boy. The thought of grabbing the child, if he were spotted, was quickly dismissed. There was still activity on the deck overhead.

Come on, kid, go home, he prayed. You must be gettin' bored by now. Not so; the child was now experimenting, sailing the wood, nudging his primitive craft through the water. This was a more dangerous activity, causing the boy to move sideways, first away from the dock and then back in Ramsey's direction.

If he comes under here I've got to take him, resolved the silent man. But then there would be a search, surely before dark. Jesus, no options, he conceded. The boy, tired of his game, straightened and threw the stick far out into the river. He watched for a moment, turned, and was gone.

Ramsey let the tension drain slowly from his body. His breathing returned to normal. He felt elated, purged, not having been forced into a situation where the boy might have become expendable.

His dark, hidden world had become strangely quiet. The overhead traffic had ceased, though he could still hear voices raised in heated discussion at the far end of the dock. Half an hour passed. More shouts, and the black hull of the junk laboriously cleared the pilings.

Ramsey waited fifteen minutes, then crawled to the upriver side of the dock. He was blinded by the harsh light. It had been a long time since his eyes had stared into the sun.

The opposite side of the river sprouted crane booms and warehouses. Freighters docked alongside wharves, swarmed with black-clad figures. Bundles of commerce, balanced precariously on backs and heads, moved up wooden gangways.

The ships were already prepared for quick departures. Smoke was expelled in spasmodic bursts from their stacks. The city followed the curve of the river, swinging to the left. The view of the span, carrying the coastal highway traffic, was obscured by the end of the river's course.

The south side of the river, where he was hidden, consisted of rude shacks marching down to the water's edge. These were the homes of the laborers whose toil kept the heart of the city pumping. The concrete two-story apartments behind the docks and cranes on the other side probably housed the bureaucrats and civil servants of the regime.

The river was laden with commerce. Ramsey contemplated the results of an airstrike and knew the consequences would be devastating. Why don't we do it? he wondered. All this shit that's movin' is being used against us, or at least supporting Charlie in the South. Those stupid shits in Washington don't understand fuck all, he raged.

On his side of the river muddy paths wound between the squalid huts. Half-naked children were the only humans visible in the steaming, bright landscape. Anyone over the age of twelve would be conscripted into the war effort. He was somehow depressed by the whole scene. Retreating to the boat, he folded himself into the bottom and tried to fall asleep.

Exhausted, he hung suspended in a semiconscious zone. The noise of the river and the city filtered through the haze behind his eyes. Another junk arrived and was quickly loaded by sweating deckhands toiling in the late-afternoon sun. Dark clouds were building over the mountains, harbingers of the coming rain.

Ramsey awoke, the black mood still hovering around his head. I'm like a friggin' manic depressive, he thought, emotions churning an empty stomach. 'Course some food would help; he smiled sardonically, catching the scent of wood smoke from early-evening cooking fires drifting over the river bank.

He moodily contemplated the dirty brown water rippling around the pilings. The tide was coming in. He could tell by the direction of turbulence surrounding the dock supports. It would be at least four hours until he could begin again, carried by the outgoing tide. Another depressing prospect, more waiting, time slowly dragging.

The rain arrived without warning. Huge drops sending out circles over the water's surface. Then faster, in a steady rhythm, until the whole river seemed to be dancing and jumping. There had been no dusk, no gradual fading of light. The shroud of darkness was in place, complete.

The temperature dropped. Ramsey shivered, water dripping all around, finding the spaces between the boards overhead. Anger and frustration were accumulating, his only thought to be rid of this place, be on his way, moving again.

He began to breathe slowly and deeply. He emptied his cluttered mind and stared unseeing into the murky depths of the night. Motionless, his chest rose and fell with ever-decreasing cadence until it seemed the figure was lifeless, hewn from rock.

His spirit soared away, flashing across a crackling glacier, over a spine of misty pinnacles, down, down to traverse the glass surface of a mountain lake. On and on, drawn along the fiery, shimmering path cast by the rising sun. Now emerald forests, giant legions marching off to the horizon, broken only by silvery dabs of mercury lakes, glistening through the ranks.

The mystical spirit slowed, descending into a fjord booming and thundering, filled with sea mist. Spiraling, twisting down the length between the craggy faces, bursting out to the open sea. The spirit silently folded its wings and dropped, plummeting into dark oblivion.

Ramsey opened his eyes and immediately checked the flow of the tide. It was full and beginning to turn.

He ignored the persistent ache deep in his belly and began to make ready for the sea. He was in an absolute black vacuum, no sound except the drumming of the rain.

Two feet from his face a raised hand became invisible. Ramsey felt around the bottom until he encountered the paddle. Ankle-deep in the black mud, he pushed off and swung the bow around. The boat began to drift sideways. He was not aware of the movement until a shadowy piling rose out of the gloom alongside the gunwale. He paddled on the starboard side, counteracting the current.

He was able to maintain position underneath what he judged to be the middle of the dock. He wanted to be well out into the river before turning seaward—his chances of grounding on a point or wharf would be less.

Rain hammered his head and shoulders. He was out from under the wharf. Another twenty or thirty yards and he would let the boat be carried by the tide. Water was everywhere, rolling down his face, slopping into the boat. He blinked his eyes rapidly to clear his already impaired vision.

Occasional flashes of light radiated out from the shore, only to be diffused by the wall of rain. Perhaps a welder's torch, or an opening door, sending proof of human habitation through the primeval darkness.

Ramsey stopped paddling. The bow swung, seeking the road to the sea. "Okay, baby, let's do it," he spoke aloud, addressing the little boat amidst the torrent. "Now we know how old Noah felt, don't we?" He could see nothing beyond a small circle of river encompassing the boat.

The water in the bottom was lapping around his ankles. His feet were numb and his lower legs ached, courtesy of leather straps with which he had been bound in the early days of captivity. He wiggled his toes in an attempt to restore circulation.

A sharp pain in his left foot caused him to gasp. Examining the sole, he found a fishbone imbedded in the skin. Ramsey held the offending fragment before his eyes, all that the rats had left. Leaning out over the side, his face not six inches from the surface, he dropped the bone into the river. The bone sank slowly, but not before Ramsey was able to gauge the speed of his craft.

He was satisfied with the progress of his journey to the sea. There was no point to raising the sail. The rain came straight down, smothering any movement of wind. The persistent thrumming of the rain on his unprotected head and an empty stomach combined to produce a dizzy, floating sensation.

A surge of paranoia swept over him. He imagined a great bow wave from a freighter engulfing his boat. That was how it would end, huge propellers sucking his body under, grinding and chopping. He probed the darkness, seeking running lights, navigational aids. Nothing, a black cloak of despair.

He wrapped his arms tightly around himself and crouched, miserable and freezing, on the floorboards. He willed himself to endure perhaps an hour in this position. Swiftly as it had arrived, the rain abruptly ended.

An eerie silence embraced the river. The mist, stirred lazily by the light wind, meandered seaward. The water was becoming choppy. The little craft rose and bounced, now slipping sideways. The river mouth, he sensed it at once, realizing the turbulence was the meeting place.

By touch and holding the rigging a few inches from his face, he made ready the sail and mast. Fumbling and cursing, he struggled for what seemed to be an hour before the sail billowed out on a starboard tack.

The dark cloud hanging around his head dissipated. The bow made headway, reaching for the broad expanse of ocean. A precursor of good fortune, the sky behind was brightening, clouds breaking up and advancing out over the sea.

Ramsey was elated, moving again, doing something. The buoyancy allowed him to subdue the physical torment exuded by nearly every portion of his body. Even the hunger seemed of little consequence. He had gone beyond the point of ravenous desire. He now felt only emptiness.

He had for some time avoided any assessment of his condition. He refused to consider that limbs or organs might cease to function. Actually, he was afraid of what he might be forced to accept.

Shafts of moonlight through the broken overcast permitted a cursory examination. He looked with disgust at his swollen feet. The tops and all around the ankles were raw and red, crisscrossed by welts and oozing cuts. Picking dead white puckered skin from the soles, he was reminded of soggy bread.

Those portions of his legs not covered by the remnants of his prison garb were dotted by boils and open sores. His crotch and rear were likewise infected, causing constant burning and itching. He was able to circle his wrists with thumb and forefinger touching. Elbows and ribs stretched the surface of his skin taut. Jungle-sore rings overspread his chest and back.

To an observer, the face would appear to be that of a cadaver. Only the eyes burned fanatically from a gray, stubbled visage with cavernous sockets. Ramsey ran his tongue over split lips, then probed his remaining teeth. Half of them rocked back and forth in the cracked gums. "Shit, I sure ain't no candidate for Mr. America," he addressed the wasted body.

Dismissing the results of his inspection, he turned his mind to other complexities. He swiveled from the tiller seat, seeking his bearings. The bulk of the land outlined against the sky fell gradually away. He was well clear of the river mouth.

He concentrated on sailing the boat, trimming the sail to attain maximum speed. His best course was east southeast, almost directly perpendicular, away from the coast. So be it, he thought, I'll take my chances on the blue water. No more scrabblin' around like a fuckin' rat. Good-by, land, we're outward bound.

He settled in to what he hoped would be four or five hours of steady sailing. The wind would probably die before dawn. By that time he could, if all went according to plan, be some ten to twelve miles offshore.

The chop had given way to long rolling swells. The sailing was comfortable and pleasant. Stars were now visible through ever-increasing gaps overhead. Arrows of light pierced through the clouds and dappled the surface of the sea. The lights of a ship far off on the horizon raised his spirits even more. Something thumped against the hull and splashed back into the water. Ramsey figured a flying fish. He hoped others might make a similar mistake and land in the boat.

He considered breaking out the net and streaming it over the stern. This would slow the boat down and divert his attention from sailing. He was determined to put as much distance as possible between himself and the enemy.

"Wait till dawn," he cautioned. "I'll be able to see better and a few more hours won't matter." Ramsey started. He realized he was talking to himself again.

He ascribed his ramblings to lack of food and sleep. He was indeed fuzzy and detached. Apprehension and concern nudged his mind. He strove to clarify his thinking.

In times of stress, or to reassure himself of his abilities and sanity, he would vocalize thoughts and feelings. This practice had begun after the torture was initiated. In the beginning he had not been tortured. Certainly the majority of his first two weeks had been spent in the cage.

The real privation was not being able to establish contact with other prisoners. This was necessary to determine what was expected, to find out who was the senior man and the policy of resistance. Ramsey was on his own and would therefore follow his personal code of behavior.

There were the occasional kicks and punches and, of course, Tran's subtle interrogations, plus the nightly propaganda sessions. The requests for information and cooperation became more insistent. Hints that other prisoners had provided information were supported by signed statements shown to him. American voices, reading obviously distorted news and propaganda, issued daily from the camp's primitive speaker system.

Ramsey had observed signs of resistance, but now he was fed all this information to the contrary. He gave nothing. He wanted to be able to face himself for the rest of his life. So resolved, he anticipated himself ready for whatever they might throw his way. The first night with the rats had unnerved him but he recovered, accepting them as a fact of life in the cage....

22
TORTURE

LATE IN the evening they came for him. He was taken to a room in back of the main building. It appeared to be an afterthought, tacked on to the rear without concern for windows or ventilation. The room was small and stifling hot. A single dim bulb was suspended on a cord from the middle of the ceiling. A wooden stool stood beneath the light.

The two guards sat him on the stool and placed themselves on either side. Tran's shadowed figure leaned against the opposite wall. Nothing happened for the first ten minutes. Ramsey sat, tensed, expecting at any second the first blow. He knew this was it. The session designed to prove that cooperation was tantamount to survival.

The anticipation was agony. Sweat bathed his whole body. The wounded leg ached and trembled. How would they do it? Ramsey wondered. He choked back the urge to speak, make a joke, anything. The silence was deadly. To Ramsey, the sound of his own breathing filled the room.

Tran's eyes appeared to be closed. An image of a snake, lazily preparing to strike a cornered quarry. "The name of your commanding officer?" The question came like an exploding mortar round on the stillness of the room.

Ramsey shook his head. A stunning blow to his right ear sent him toppling from the stool. He lay on the floor, his ear ringing. The guards dragged him back to his seat. "His name, Ramsey?" The shake of the head, same result, only this time the left side.

Back on the stool, his head pounding, he prepared for the next onslaught. "Go ahead, fuckers, hammer me, you get nothin'. You're pissin' me off." The words belied his actual sense of helplessness. His pronouncement bounced off the sweating walls and fell empty to the floor.

"The name?" The tone unchanged, monotonous, bored, in no hurry. Time meant nothing. The jaw was the target of the guard's club. Lying on the floor once again, Ramsey spat blood and shards of teeth into the dust.

He refused to move by himself. Make them exert themselves, no help from here, was his silent pledge. He hung like a corpse between them until he was placed on the stool. The room was rotating around the edge of his vision. His head felt ready to burst like a ripe watermelon.

"Ramsey, please do not think me impatient. We can do this forever. I am only thinking of your welfare. This punishment is only the beginning. Everyone cooperates, as you will." Ramsey was grateful for Tran's speech. It gave him a little time to recoup his losses.

"Is it too much to ask why I'm being punished in the first place?" He was surprised by the croaking sound of his voice. The sarcasm he intended did not come across.

"You are a war criminal. The name, please." Tran would not be put off from his objective.

Ramsey did not shake his head; it hurt too much. He sat silently, hands hanging between his thighs. The heel of a hand was driven savagely into the base of his skull. White lights detonated behind his eyes. He was propelled forward, his face colliding with the rising floor.

The guards were on him, using feet and clubs. He refused to cry out. He clenched his teeth, curled into a ball, and cupped his hands protectively between his legs. His body, already wracked by pain and exhaustion, was numb. Their blows made little impression. They seemed to be coming from far, far away. The sound of his flesh being abused was worse than the actual pain of the impact.

He was going under when they stopped. Vaguely, he felt himself lifted and the hard wood of the stool come in contact with his buttocks. His head hung forward. He noted with interest drops of blood from his battered face dripping and splashing intricate patterns in the dust.

Tran's voice cut through the protective fog cradling his brain. "The name of your commanding officer?" Ramsey felt the anger charging up his throat. "Jesus, change the record!" The hoarse words were out before he could close his lips.

Silence, no retaliation, the guards remained passive. Ramsey was puzzled. Maybe they're tired and want to go home and snuggle up with the wife. His thoughts were becoming increasingly bizarre.

Tran fired off a command. The guards left the room. The interrogator returned to his position against the wall. Before Ramsey had a chance to ponder these latest developments, the guards returned. They brought with them an assortment of ropes and straps.

Ramsey's arms were seized and jerked behind his back. They were bound together at the elbow and wrist. The bindings were excruciatingly tight and almost at once tore into his flesh. A foot in the back drove him from the stool. His legs were now strapped at the ankles and knees.

He was placed in the sitting position. The guard he came to know later as Oahn jerked his wrists up toward the ceiling. His head was forced down, almost touching his knees. A loop of rope was passed around his neck and legs.

At first the pain was not extreme. His body was still numb from the beating and the ropes cutting off circulation. Ten minutes later he was screaming in agony. He couldn't help himself. Never had he felt such blinding pain. Rivers of fire coursed through his veins and exploded like napalm at each joint of his body.

They thrust a rag into his mouth to silence the screams. He vomited. Bile spewed from his nose and backed up in his throat. He was dying, choking in his own vomit. The rag was removed. The vile fluid gushed over his chest. His empty stomach continued to heave and convulse.

His entire body shook.

He lost control of his bowels. The agony was so great, he felt no humiliation. He bit through his lip to stifle the screams. The salty blood filled his mouth and the screams were silent, inside his head.

Ramsey knew it was almost over; he couldn't take much more. He prayed for unconsciousness, but the pain was too great. Through a red haze he heard from afar, "Will you answer my question now? You will be released if you agree." Ramsey dumbly nodded his head.

The guards untied the ropes. He lay in his own

stench and vomit. "The name, Ramsey." Tran's voice was soft, intimate. What the fuck is the big deal, Ramsey seethed. Anger replaced the shame he had begun to feel. Why are they going to such lengths for a piece of trivial information?

"The name, please." Again the low insistent tone. A shaft of understanding finally pierced Ramsey's muddled brain. They don't care, he knew it now. They really don't give a shit. Tran probably knows the answer already. It's me they want. Break me, break me to prove it can be done, to set me straight that no one can resist for long.

His fury was released, giving him the will to resist. Screw them, he smoldered. "Fuck off, I changed my mind!" He spat into the putrid dust. Tran sighed, then gave the command. The guards bound him once again, and if it were possible, tighter than before.

Once again the rag was inserted. They left the room without a word. The pain was immediate. He thrashed his head from side to side in an attempt to dislodge the rag. His throat was sandpaper. He coughed and gagged. The cloth was expelled to the sound of his screams.

Ramsey rolled to the side and methodically beat his head on the floor. Reason was draining away. The dull thud of his head against the floor echoed in his ears. Blood drained and sprinkled in the dust each time he raised his head. He sobbed and screamed amidst the slime of his body fluids coating the floor.

Mercifully, his body decided he had suffered enough and shut down. Even in the unconscious state Ramsey continued to jerk and convulse as if immersed in some grotesque nightmare. How long he lay in his stupor he could not guess. When he awoke, they were in the room.

"The name, Ramsey." More a command than a question. "I can't, I can't," he sobbed. "Can't you understand that, you fuckin' dog?" The insult was hurled with Ramsey's last remaining strength. He knew that to Tran it was an extremely derogatory affront to be labeled as such. The door slammed behind their receding steps.

The pain was not so extreme. His hands, legs, and feet were swollen. Time ceased. He could not distinguish what was real and what was imaginary. He could hear the sound of his own sobbing, but it seemed to come from behind a curtain.

The terror and pain he felt produced hallucinations filled with blood and broken bodies. Dimly he wondered in a moment of clarity if they had given him drugs. I'm goin' to have to give them something, he conceded. Either they'll kill me or I'll kill myself.

He felt totally alone, cut off from the human race, involved in some horrible rite of sacrifice. The door slammed open. Through swollen eyes he saw Tran's dusty boots before his face. The guards wore rubber-tire sandals. Incredibly, they began to untie the ropes.

His joy and soaring spirits were quickly dispelled.

The circulation returned to his tormented limbs. He writhed and flopped like a wounded animal hearing its death knell. A million hot needles were plunged into his flesh. He made guttural sobbing and groaning noises but would not scream.

The guards heaved him up onto the stool. His spine and brain seemed to be the only functioning portions of his anatomy. His feet and legs would not move. They were splayed out before him like those belonging to a rag doll. His hands hung useless at the ends of arms he could not raise.

He slumped on the stool, a picture of utter dejection, blood and vomit smeared across his chest and thighs. The ember was dying. Try as he might, Ramsey could not push back the darkness. He was slipping into oblivion where there was no pain or terror.

"Ramsey, look at me." Tran was in his old position against the wall. "We have been at this for only a short time. We can continue indefinitely, until you are either dead or a vegetable. Do you wish that upon yourself? Ah, you do not care to reply to that question. Perhaps then you will please answer my original request." The spark flickered and danced.

Ramsey could not get enough saliva into his parched throat and mouth. The sound was like a rusty nail pulled from a board, but the intent was clear. "Screw you!" Tran stormed from the room, leaving the guards to secure the ropes. The light was extinguished.

He was alone in the darkness. Great clouds of mosquitoes and other insects honed in on his blood. They swarmed about him, biting, stinging, and crawling into his nose and ears.

Get through the next minute, he told himself, then the next five minutes. He pictured himself, outside of his body, sitting against the wall observing the tormented mess huddled on the floor. Dispassionately he counseled the figure, You can't go on. Give them something, then fall back.

The sobbing man's fears were hurled across the room. But once I start, they'll have me. I won't be able to stop. Tell lies, the apparition advised. To be broken means you cooperate fully. You are in their power and they can get anything they want. If you give false information, you are fighting them, understand?

Once again the door swung open. Tran was silhouetted against the night sky. How long had he been in the ropes? Ramsey had no concept of the passage of time. It could have been an hour, six hours, a day. The figure in the door was motionless, silent. The door closed slowly and he was gone.

Ramsey felt an overwhelming urge to call out, to bring him back. Low, moaning animal sounds escaped involuntarily from his throat. Well fuck it, fuck it, that's what he wants me to do. Make me call him and beg the little shit to let me talk.

Again the anger gave him strength and a period

of rational thought. I've gotta get out of this. I'm no good the way I am. The words trailed through his brain. He lost consciousness once more, or perhaps it was sleep creeping in to mask the agony.

He came painfully awake to noises outside the room. His first thoughts attempted to diffuse the reality of his circumstances. It's a bad dream, a nightmare. It's not really happening. I'll wake up soon and be someplace safe. Tears squeezed from eyes screwed shut against pain and the room.

The opening poured in sunlight. The foul room and its occupant were illuminated. Tran's face wrinkled in disgust. He tapped the swollen body with his boot. "A sorry state, Ramsey. But I suppose the punishment befits a criminal who is not willing to repent. It is going to be a terribly long day for you, I'm afraid, unless there is something you wish to say."

The gory head nodded slightly. He was untied. The three enemies watched with indifference. He fought the pain and nausea suffusing his body. He was placed on the stool once more. He swayed back and forth, struggling for balance.

"The name of your commanding officer?" This time, the gentle persuasive voice. Ramsey licked his lips. They felt strangely foreign, removed from his body. He bobbed his head, making swallowing motions. He pointed down his throat, opening and closing his mouth.

It was contrived. He had decided, even if he told

them lies, they were going to provide something in return. Tran gave an order. A guard returned moments later with a canteen cup of water. Ramsey's arms were useless. The guard fed him the tepid water.

It was the most glorious liquid he had ever tasted. He continued with exaggerated swallowing motions, stalling, gaining time. Tran shifted impatiently. "Your answer." Ramsey made a pretense of gaining his composure. The image of a man reluctant, but about to compromise himself.

"Captain Jack Spratt is my commanding officer." He enunciated carefully, hoping the interrogator was not a nursery rhyme aficionado. The lie was passed over. "How many teams such as yours are operating in northern Quang Tri Province and across the border?"

The question came rapidly on the heels of his answer. Ramsey had no idea, but knew a number was wanted. "Twenty-five," he answered, supplying his house address.

"Excellent. Now describe your mission and the objectives of the other teams."

Tran was on a roll. Ramsey stopped him dead. "As a fellow soldier, you must know my honor will not allow me to discuss this subject." He hoped to maneuver the interrogator into a position that might cause him to lose face should he demand further answers. The question of honor and face would be a sensitive area for Tran.

Ramsey pressed on, taking advantage of the silence. "Besides, I feel that enough has been said today. I have cooperated and answered your questions." He held his breath, the silence expanding, filling the room. Tran ended the tension, growling some orders to the guards.

He was dragged from the room, helpless feet digging furrows across the compound. Back in his cell, he was given some cold soup. The guard, a veteran of these sessions, had placed the bowl on the floor. He knew Ramsey could not hold the container. He slid painfully across the floor and lapped the soup like a dog.

The irony of the situation cracked his face in a brief smile. He had called Tran a dog and now here he was, behaving like one. He was deeply troubled and ashamed. Even though he had given nothing, he felt as if he had betrayed his code. He had gone beyond the pieces of information required. He had talked to the enemy.

Ramsey wondered about the other prisoners. What had they given? Had they been hard-liners and held out? Was he a weak sister? On the other hand, he had made it through. He had not given up anything of value except his own conviction that he could resist.

He stared moodily into the empty bowl and made his resolve. I will go as far as I can each time, then I will lie. I will give them nothing they can use. I will sign nothing. I will not make any statements. With this promise, he mended his shattered illusions.

It would be some time before he discovered that everyone in the camp had been broken in various degrees. A few prisoners had gone over the edge completely and now cooperated wholeheartedly with the enemy. The majority resisted to the best of their ability.

It was three days before he regained the use of his limbs. Both his hands and feet remained swollen and discolored for almost two weeks. The rope scars would remain with him always.

There were two other sessions like the first. Ramsey held out as long as possible, then supplied ludicrous information. Again, Tran did not appear to be concerned with the knowledge, but rather with the process of making him talk.

Tran continued to press for documents or tapes. Ramsey was adamant. He would have preferred death. The interrogator sensed this feeling and in his own way understood. However, when his superiors demanded fodder for the propaganda machine, he would renew his efforts, threatening the ropes....

23
THE DREAM FULFILLED

Now on the open sea, Ramsey congratulated himself on his behavior and resistance. He had made it through intact. His body had suffered greatly but would mend with time. More significant was the fact that in his concept of self, he was stronger than ever.

The land was a broken smudge, darker than the clearing sky. A thin silver bow of moon hung amid a blue-black tapestry of stars. The wind still held and the little boat plowed steadily onward. Rolling and immense, the sea was alive with creature noises.

Ramsey could hear the whir and splash of flying fish. Occasionally he heard a noise akin to that of a low grunting or moaning. In the lazy wake of the boat he glimpsed a dorsal fin crossing his track. Tiny phosphorescent organisms streamed past the boat.

He continued to converse with himself, fighting the weakness of his body and the inability of his mind to focus steadily on the predicament at hand. "Come on, Ramsey, you're in the home stretch now. Square away, get your act together."

He dozed, the tiller clamped tightly under his arm. The flapping of the sail awoke him and the heading was corrected. His course became more erratic. The ability to fight against a slumbering brain slowly drained away.

Leaning far out over the side, he immersed his head in the sea. Somewhat revived, he cast about looking for something to occupy his mind and hands. "I've gotta do something, anything to stay awake." The words were confirmed by the slow-motion movement of his limbs.

The fishing net caught his attention. Clumsily he spread the bundle, draping the material over the seat and floorboards.

An idea began to take shape. With stiff and fumbling fingers he began to untie the various trailing lines. He worked steadily, pushing back the frustration that mounted each time he tackled a knot.

Ramsey then attached a line to each corner of the

net. He lowered the net over the stern, weighted side first, and let the lines out slowly. The net would act like a large sea anchor. But it was better than the impossible task of casting from a moving boat.

The boat slowed against the drag of the net but still made headway. He could see the cork floats bobbing along the surface twenty feet behind. He secured the lines on either side of the stern.

If he was lucky, the net would retain its rectangular shape and, in passing through the water, snare an unsuspecting meal. He had to steer more carefully now. The drag of the net had a tendency to pull the bow into the wind.

Ramsey was slightly rejuvenated by the activity and was able to sail competently for an hour. It was close to dawn. The sky above the horizon was the hue of a pearl. Ramsey was fading again, sliding gently down, reaching for the beckoning arms of comfort.

The stern was violently wrenched to the right. Trailing ropes sprang clear of the water, quivering with tension, spraying droplets into the air. The length of the boat quivered under Ramsey's feet. A wild thrashing erupted in the water behind the craft. The ropes hummed with strain. All forward motion ceased.

He tried to untie the ropes, but the pressure of the knots was too great. He saw a deadly torpedo shape lighter than the dark swirl of the sea. The brute's head slashed from side to side, tearing at the net with rows of triangular teeth. A cold unblinking eye focused balefully on him, forecasting impending doom.

He could do nothing but watch and pray the shark would vent its rage on the net and nothing else. The gunwale dipped down to the surface of the sea. Ramsey grabbed the mast, hanging on as the boat rocked, shipping water. The blunt head turned and charged toward the boat. The great jaws wide, the gleaming teeth, festooned with rope, came crunching down on the steering oar and stern. The wood exploded and splintered, flying through the air like so much chaff.

Half the transom was gone, a shattered tooth embedded in the remaining portion. Ramsey was drenched by spray, the shark rolling and diving away. One of the ropes was severed, the other still taut. The boat was dragged in a half circle though the boiling water. With a long rending crack, the wooden cleat securing the rope ripped away and vanished into the sea.

The turmoil subsided, the remains of the boat and man rocking gently. He searched the surface, fearing at any moment another attack by the marauder. The fin appeared, off to his right, and began a lazy circle. Ramsey's thudding heart slowed and he finally exhaled.

Warily checking the fin, he used his hands to paddle the bow around until the sail would fill. Once more a decision had been made, taken out of his hands. The tiller gone, his course would be left to the vagaries of the wind. A steady, gentle breeze carried him on, ever to the southeast.

Ramsey scanned the boat, seeking a makeshift

tiller or paddle. The only possibility was the seat in the stern. Even then, it was too short for a tiller, but at least it would serve as a primitive paddle. Kneeling, he banged up with clenched fists, trying to dislodge the wood from four rusty screws.

His weakness surprised him. Trembling and light headed from exertion, he abandoned the effort. He sat gazing at his shaking hands, overcome with nausea. Dimly he became aware of warmth washing over his body. The slitted eyes rose to the inflamed horizon.

A red, shimmering sun expanded across the surface of the sea. Shafts of fiery luminescence streaked across the ocean's face, reaching for the boat. The dawn surged upon a tranquil world. The wind was gradually dying.

Ramsey roused himself, thinking, no food, no water, no tiller; but at least he had the sun. A few hours later the welcome rays had turned to lances of affliction. No wind, the superheated air embracing him like a steaming blanket.

The searing light bounced off the oily sea and the white cloth of the sail. His eyes baked within their sockets. He sought refuge, lying on the floorboards, shaded by the sail. Still he burned, the already dehydrated body yielding its precious fluids.

With each passing hour the sun rose higher, the heat intensifying. His cracked lips sought the stagnant rainwater between the floorboards. It was brackish and oily, contaminated by seawater. Still, he swallowed the moisture. The relief was temporary. Soon his throat ached and his tongue felt twice its normal size.

He dropped the useless sail and covered his burning body from head to foot. He could do nothing more. He could only endure. He knew if he were going to be found, it would have to be soon. In his pitifully weakened state the ability to retain sanity and resist the leering face of death would gradually slip away.

In all of the journey he had never felt so helpless, so removed from his surroundings. He was a body beneath a shroud, awaiting a verdict by the forces of the universe. The little craft rotated under the furnace of the sky.

Still the sun relentlessly pursued its course, now directly overhead. Over the far land black clouds boiled and lashed with torrential rains. Not so on the burning sea. Within his cocoon, Ramsey scarcely moved, the rapid rising and falling of his chest the only evidence that life tenaciously clung to the decimated frame.

By the middle of the afternoon he had ceased to think. It was too much effort, reality was pain and anguish. Better to drift in a neutral, uncomplicated state of nothingness. His skin was burning and clammy, having sweated out the extent of its moisture.

Black spots circled the parameters of his vision. At times he felt enclosed by intense white heat, his body about to burst into flames. Then blackness would descend, a hot sulfurous breath fanned across his floating corpse. The indifferent sun gravitated toward the line of the horizon. Slowly, reluctantly it hung, then plummeted, leaving a savage glow to mark the passage of day.

Night began its rule over the tranquil sea. The little craft rose and fell, a dot on the great circle round. The coming of darkness drew no response from the man. He was only minutely aware of his body contracting and shaking with the cooling of the air. Otherwise, he hung suspended in some ethereal air.

He was likewise unaware of a friendly patrol craft passing a mile to seaward. The cutter was headed north, its mission to deter or disrupt enemy coastal activity. Clouds racing over the face of the moon hid Ramsey's little boat, making it one with the dark sea swell.

The drone of powerful engines faded into the night. Ramsey's brain was silently alarmed by the widening gulf between itself and the body. The impulses and alarms generated no response. Air and blood still arrived, but the supply was diminishing and irregular.

The mechanism reduced activity, protecting the thin connecting gossamer thread of life. The sea rolled on beneath a circle-studded sky, cradling a frail human to its ancient bosom. The darkness covering half the world slowly receded.

Once again booming up from the rim of the earth came the light. Ramsey was warm and comfortable, sundered from the physical confines of his body. An aura of wholeness, of being an ingredient, diffused his form. He was a microorganism of the sea, a zephyr of wind, a glimmer of sunlight. He was all things from the loam of the earth to the infinite reaches of the universe.

The configuration under the sailcloth was motionless. The little boat, like a homeless nomad, wandered across the dawn-smeared sea. Ramsey was free. The odyssey finished. The dream fulfilled....

24
THE CUTTER, VIGILANT

BOATSWAIN'S MATE Neilsen rubbed his grainy, aching eyes. Another long night in a succession of mostly fruitless patrols. Their mission was to intercept supplies headed south by sea. His watch was almost over. Gratefully he cradled the steaming coffee.

The deck vibrated beneath his feet, powerful engines driving the ship homeward. Neilsen was a conscientious seaman; he considered his contribution to the war a serious business. So now, even in the waning moments before relief, he continued to scan each point of the compass.

Initially he thought it was a black spot swimming before his tired eyes. Then it steadied and settled into a discernible shape. Neilsen indicated to the helmsman, "Two points off the starboard bow." He cut back the throttles and rang down for the skipper.

The bow swung, the cutter dropped lower in the water at reduced speed. "What's up, Neilsen?" The skipper was behind him, clad only in khaki shorts. "Boat, sir, dead in the water. Too small to be out here. Thought we'd take a look-see."

The lieutenant nodded. "Okay, take her in slow. Sound general quarters. Can't be too careful. It could be booby-trapped." The Klaxon shattered the morning calm, sending the crew scrambling to battle stations.

Neilsen slowed the ship's forward progress even more, the little boat now forty yards away. "Circle around while we scope it out." Neilsen detected in the skipper's voice a tenseness he himself felt. Anything out of the ordinary deserved suspicion and caution.

The cutter described a circle. The little craft bobbed in the turbulence. "Get us in closer, Neilsen. There's somethin' in the bottom." He peered through the binoculars, a frown wrinkled across his brow. The silence lengthened, punctuated by the low throb of the engines.

"Jesus, there's someone under that canvas! I can see a foot. All stop!" Neilsen jammed the levers into neutral. The lieutenant was now out on deck. "You men, keep your weapons trained on that bundle. Rosario, get a hook on that boat!"

The sailor extended a long boat gaff and hooked a gunwale. He gradually drew the boat alongside the cutter. The majority of the crew had moved to the rail, weapons still raised. Still no movement from beneath the sailcloth. A filthy, scrawny foot was the only evidence of a human form.

"Rosario, see if you can lift the canvas." The hook tentively probed and caught a corner. The shroud was lifted and flopped back to reveal the occupant. Huddled in the fetal position, the body was blistered and blackened. Scraps of cloth hung around the emaciated waist.

"Skipper, this guy is one of us!" The face of the body displayed a slight smile of calm repose. "Put a ladder over. Let's get the poor bastard on board."

Two seamen dropped into the boat, carefully avoiding the body. They did not relish the grisly task of wrapping the corpse in its covering. Straddling the head, one of the sailors held his breath against the rancid odor and bent to the task. He abruptly straightened, eyes wide and incredulous, staring at the crew. "This guy is alive! This guy is alive!"

25
REQUIEM

EARLY-MORNING light softened the harsh lines of the granite blocks. The great city was hushed. Occasionally the murmur of automobile or bus would intrude upon the quiet of the dawn.

He had risen in darkness, unable to dispel the apprehension and emotional upheaval curdling in his stomach. A sense of foreboding, a flickering of hope, what did he hope to find here? An explanation perhaps, a thread of meaning stretching across the void of his past.

The pictures had touched him in a manner he had not thought possible. His cynical veneer had been splintered by images of ragged men reaching out with shaking hands. The candid tears eroded his resolve to remain aloof and isolated from causes and movements.

The inexplicable emotion, the binding together of raw, dark wounds had been there, reaching out, penetrating his soul. The screen blurred. He made no attempt to wipe the tears or stifle the convulsive sobs. He wept for all he had lost—the innocence, the love, the man he had once believed in and accepted.

It was then he knew the journey must be made. The purge was incomplete. He knew he must go and touch and experience the place, and in so doing illuminate the smothering darkness.

Jenny understood his need to make the journey alone. She had been awed by the depth of his response to the dedication ceremonies. This controlled, strong-willed man she had lived with for years had been torn apart like a grieving child. He was tender, yes, sometimes even sentimental, but she had never pierced the thick shell surrounding his past.

In spite of the love she felt, he frightened her. He would withdraw for days at a time, closing her out. He kept his distance, a silent, brooding man lost with his own thoughts. Perhaps this journey would make a difference. It was, she hoped, a beginning.

Ramsey's face shimmered on the polished stone.

The tentative winter sun reflected an expressionless mask. It had been an hour. He had not moved. He stood rigid, fists clenched by his side. The epic of names swam before his eyes. He could not bring himself to move forward.

The creeping shadow of the Washington Monument reached out to the lone figure. The city was coming awake in the chilled air. The business of government and commerce was underway. A thundering jet rising overhead failed to register on the ears of the solitary man. Ramsey was oblivious, secreted deep within his memories.

The years had slipped away, filled with hollow triumphs. The government and media had made him a hero. He did not want the title. A life had been established, hanging on the edge of normalcy. He had returned to college and then secured a job as an investigative reporter. Jenny was the stabilizing factor. She was a barometer of his moods, reacting and fluctuating with the flow. Could he have made it without her? How had it all begun?...

The bar in Laguna was a local hangout, dimly lit and comfortable. Regulars in workclothes lined the rail, hoisting beers and occasional shots of whiskey. Opposite the bar, narrow wooden booths made up the other wall. A television with poor reception glimmered above the sweating bartender. Ramsey ordered a beer. "You want a glass with that?"

Now there's a decision I can handle, he thought. "Naw, that's all right. Can I get a sandwich?"

"You gotta sit in a booth for that. Waitress be around eventually."

Ramsey raised his bottle. "Thanks, no hurry."

The regulars began to drift out, family obligations disrupting the bar's male camaraderie. He received a few curious glances, but little else. The waitress had been friendly. He chewed thoughtfully, following her with his eyes. She was definitely interesting. A little heavy, perhaps, but with pale, translucent skin. She moved gracefully, long shining black hair swinging with her movements. She had smiled at him, large brown eyes hinting, perhaps. Or was it just her way?

He felt himself stir. His stomach sank toward his groin. A warm yearning flooded through his body. God, it's been a long time, he mused.

"Another beer, fella?"

"Yes, please." Was it his imagination or was there an extra swing to her hips as she turned toward the bar?

Smiling gently into her eyes, he asked, "What's your name?"

"Jenny. What's yours?"

"Jack. Nice to meet you." She caught his eyes straying to the curve of breast pushing against the fabric of her blouse.

He took a swig of beer to hide his embarrassment. Her laugh was a husky rumble. "Talk to you later."

In the next few minutes they made eye contact several times. He signaled for another beer. She placed the frosty bottle before him and leaned over, her face close. "Slow down, honey, I don't get off till ten."

He shifted from her wide generous mouth to the laughing eyes. He toasted her with the bottle. "I'll be fine. I got a lot of wasted time to make up. I don't want to miss any of it."

He inhaled her scent and basked in her pure female presence. His nerves were jumping, begging him to pull her into the booth and explore the hills and valleys of her body. He bit down hard on the neck of the beer bottle. He was ecstatic, smiling at the smoky room, feeling the juices of life flow through his veins.

She was gone. Impulsively he stood and made his way to the telephone booth at the rear. The old wooden folding doors refused to close completely. He contemplated the phone, conscious of country western seeping in around the corners of his mind.

He wiped a sweaty palm across his shirt front and picked up the receiver. The familiar number went clicking across the continent. He hung up. Head bowed, he told himself, It's a dream. Let it die a graceful death. Ramsey beat his fist lightly against the wall. "I have to know. I have to know." He dialed again.

"Hello." The voice fired a shaft deep into his gut.

"Cathy, it's Jack." He was conscious of his every breath filling the void of silence. "Cathy?"

"Jack, is that really you? I saw you on—at the

press conference in the hospital You looked really good." She rushed on. He knew instinctively she was playing for time, gathering her thoughts. "Where are you?" she asked.

"Cathy, it's okay." His words were rational, rising over the waves of emotion pounding through his body. Again the static-filled emptiness. He had the distinct impression she was crying, her hand over the receiver.

"Oh, Jack!" He shuddered, knowing something bright and fine had been lost. "Another place, another time, Jack." She was sobbing openly now.

"Cathy, do you have any feelings of love for me?" He listened intently, hardly daring to breathe.

"You bastard, Ramsey! You bastard!" she exploded into the silence. "I'm engaged, you understand? Engaged to be married."

Eyes vacant and unfocused, he slowly put the receiver into its cradle. He stood for a long time, staring, uncomprehending, at the graffiti-scarred wall. Empty and hollow, he shuffled back to the booth.

She was there waiting. "Bad news?" He slumped back into the seat. "You wanna talk?"

He dumbly shook his head. "Maybe later, huh?" He cleared his throat. "Bring me a Scotch, just a little bit of ice. Okay?"

"You sure?"

Anger flared in his eyes. "Yes!"

Her eyes were soft. She touched his shoulder lightly.

He was on his second drink, forcing his mind to think of nothing. He concentrated on the television. Local news not good—another forest fire, more beach erosion. Then the national news. Suddenly the screen was filled with smoke. Soldiers in battle gear waded across a paddy, firing their weapons into a village.

The glass shook in his hand, rattled against the tabletop. He gripped it tighter, knuckles white against the amber liquid. A sheen of sweat coated his contorted face. He couldn't drag his eyes away. His breathing was rapid. His body rocked back and forth.

Jenny, watching him, whispered to the bartender. He reached up and switched to a western rerun. Ramsey half rose to a crouch, fists balled in anger, then slowly sank back. His hands cupped the sweating face. Tears and sweat mingled, running between his fingers. She was by his side. "Come on, let's get out of here. I can leave early."

He had no recollection of the walk back to the cottage. His next memory was of soft white skin pressed against his face. He was naked, sobs jerking and racking his body. Strong arms pulled him close. He cried unashamedly against the pillow of flesh. Then sleep, blessed at last, nothing but warmth and comfort.

He awoke to a billion stars scattered across the window canvas above the bed. The gentle murmur of the sea below sifted into the room, the soft breathing of the woman clinging to his body a fitting rhapsody to the mural.

Ramsey lay silent, afraid to disturb the communing of their bodies. He only knew he was infinitely grateful. The warmth and shape of her body was life itself. Cathy was gone. The soldiers in the paddy were gone, things of the past. This was real, a time for living. He kissed her neck, behind her ears, exulting in the chance she had given.

Anger, love, hate, sorrow—he poured it all out into the vessel of her body. It was a catharsis that shuddered into eternity. "You poor bastard, Ramsey, hold me! Hold me!" The words hammered across his brain.

The rest of the weekend passed in a dream of careless freedom. They swam, made love and made love some more, then ate and drank. Sleep was brief, an intrusion upon their explorations of each other. He discovered she had seen the press conference on television. She had known from the start who he was.

Their time together was easy. She was a totally honest person in love with life. Her appetite was voracious and sensual. Ramsey desperately needed what she had to offer. No pretense, just a plunge back into living, with a dedicated partner for participant and guide.

She drove him all the way to San Diego. They sang together with the radio and polished off two six-packs of cold beer. So he was five hours late. What were they going to do? Send him to Vietnam? Slightly high, he laughed at the thought.

The time to say good-by came all too soon. She

stood in the circle of his arms, head bowed, resting against his chest. He started to speak, struggling to express the wealth of emotion he felt. The head lifted. The eyes were shining. She placed two fingers across his lips.

"Shh, don't say anything, okay?" She kissed him quickly. "You know where to find me, Jack." She was gone, running down the stairs two at a time. Ramsey watched her swing into the car. The arm waved and was swallowed up into the night.

The old general had been sympathetic but pressed forward, adamant and persistent. Ramsey sat before the grizzled warrior, veteran of three wars. Two days after Jenny's weekend they had shipped him east to Marine Barracks, Washington, D.C.

"Listen, son, something positive has to come out of this war. The Corps must go on. We've got to have Marines like you to perpetuate the legend. We have to have kids who believe the legends and think this country is worth fighting for. Yes, even dying for."

The iron-gray crew-cut head lowered briefly as if gathering strength. "You've heard the names, I don't have to tell you: Belleau Wood, Guadalcanal, Chosin Reservoir. It's all there, pride and tradition. You heard it all in boot camp. What are we gonna tell recruits about this war?" He paused, fixing Ramsey with a questioning stare.

"Not a helluva lot, sir!" Ramsey shot back.

"You're wrong, son. We're not gonna tell them

about places or battles. We're going to tell them about people like you, Marines who did their job in spite of a shitty situation. Marines who carried on the tradition because of pride and excellence. Understand?"

Ramsey had finally capitulated and agreed to accept the medal. He had, however, wrung an agreement from the general that it was to be a one-shot deal. The ceremony would be at a regular Friday parade of the detachment and band, nothing more, no appearances or interviews.

So it came to pass on a warm summer's night in the quadrangle of the Marine Barracks. The stands were filled. The lights accentuated hues of grass, dress-blue uniforms, and brass.

Ramsey paced the squad room under the watchful eyes of his two officer escorts. The sounds of the parade carried through the open windows.

He stilled his restless body and observed the scene. The stately house of the Commandant dominated the field. Pinpoints of light flashed from instruments. Scarlet uniforms of the band contrasted vividly with the lush green grass. Marines of the detachment offered their arms, escorting ladies to their seats. It was truly impressive. He felt a surge of pride. The old truism came to mind: Once a Marine, always a Marine.

It was time. He stood between the two officers, hidden from the crowd by the overhang of the barracks. A long narrow path of bricks divided the field of green. At the far side the Sergeant Major of the

Marine Corps was reading the orders of the day. The glare of lights hid the crowded bleachers.

"Here we go, Sergeant," whispered the escort to his left. Ramsey took a breath and fell into step. They marched slowly across the field. The only sounds Ramsey could hear were the click of their polished shoes and the creak of leather. The swords of the escorts flashed with reflected light.

The order was read. Ramsey saluted. He took the box that held the medal. Handshakes, words of praise and congratulations, the salutes of dismissal. Ramsey marched to his position, willing his rigid body to function correctly.

The detachment passed in review. All was silent, the quadrangle empty. Spotlights focused on a lone, erect figure on the roof of the stone barracks. The trumpet was raised. The haunting notes of taps echoed over the field.

He had known it was coming and had fortified himself in preparation. He was not ready for the wave of sadness and remorse. It was almost a physical pain. He remained erect and stolid, but could do nothing to prevent the single threads of silver streaking down his cheeks.

He moved forward. The outstretched hand reached blindly for the names. The twisted face could not contain the tears.

There were other people now. Tourists and school

groups watching the strange figure from the corners of their eyes. He moved down the parade of tablets, fingers tracing names on the simple black granite. The polished stone pulsated with life of its own. His haggard reflection appeared to be embedded deep within the tablets. Ramsey felt an emotion he could not identify. He became as one with the names he touched. Spirits of the dead walked these grounds, mingling with the living.

There it was: James Swanson, followed by a small white cross. Unaccounted for and missing. "Oh, Swanson, you were the best and brightest we had to give." His fingers explored the indentations and curvatures of the stone. "Why am I here, and you are gone?"

Eric Wilson, small white cross. He fumbled with the buttons on his jacket. Numbed fingers drew forth the medal. How much has this cost me? he asked.

He sank to his knees, the medal a shimmering image before his eyes. He carefully placed the ribbon against the base of cold stone, midway between the names of Swanson and Wilson.

His hands struggled up, above his head, spread wide. Tears fell upon the hallowed ground, an end and a beginning.